Prospect Hill

by
Kimberly S. Seigh

PROSPECT HILL

By

Kimberly S. Seigh

To order additional copies of this book or for book publishing information, or to contact the author:

Publisher Page
P.O. Box 52
Terra Alta, WV 26764
www.publisherpage.com
www.headlinebooks.com

Tel/Fax: 800-570-5951
Email: mybook@headlinebooks.com

Publisher Page is an imprint of Headline Books, Inc.
Photographs courtesy of Cover Studio, Inc.
Newspaper excerpts courtesy of The Tribune-Democrat

ISBN—0-929915-60-7
ISBN-13—978-0929915-60-9

Library of Congress Control Number: 2007934823

PRINTED IN THE UNITED STATES OF AMERICA

Dedication

To Dearest Aunt Doll
Thank you for the stories.

Chapter One
1914

"Gertie, I had a most disturbing dream last night," said Mama.

"Tell me about it," said Gertie.

"Well, the dream started out beautifully. I was walking along a peaceful, tree-lined stream. It was lovely. Then suddenly the water in the brook began churning and bubbling violently. I heard a cry and looked into the water. There was a baby who was drowning. I ran to the water's edge and reached for the baby. I felt his wet, tiny arm. The baby slipped away. I tried again. I caught hold of the baby's ankle, but I just couldn't hold on. The baby slid away. I kept trying to save that baby. With each attempt, it became more and more difficult. The baby was getting farther and farther from me. I could not save that child."

Gertie reached for Mama's hand and said, "Your baby will be fine."

"I hope so," said Mama. "I'm sure it will be my last."

"Your baby will make ten. That is a good, round number to end with," said Gertie. "Maybe your dream was triggered by yesterday's anniversary of the Great Flood."

Mama smiled, "Perhaps you are right, my dear."

Twenty-six-year-old Gertie was the oldest of my siblings. She always knew the right thing to say to make Mama feel better. It seemed that Gertie and Mama were more like friends than mother and daughter. Gertie married a rich man who ran a copper mine in Canada. And Gertie had a baby of her own, nine-month-old Helen. Gertie and Helen had come on a train to visit us.

Gertie was right. There had been a lot of talk about floods around here. My family lived in Johnstown, Pennsylvania. There had been a terrible flood back in 1889. Over two thousand people died. People around here called it the Great Flood. Now, twenty-five years later, it was the anniversary of the catastrophe.

Unknown Plot, Johnstown, PA; over 800 unknown bodies buried of those killed in the flood, May 31, 1889.

Papa and Mama took all of us into town for a special celebration of the flood. Of course, we walked into town from our house on the hill.

"The flood was a horrible tragedy. Why are we celebrating?" asked fourteen-year-old Rudi.

"We're not celebrating the death and destruction," Papa explained. "We're celebrating the spirit of the people who rebuilt the city and carried on."

I, Crystal, was nine at the time. It was a big occasion for me to go to town. We wound our way down Washington and Market Streets before we turned onto Main Street. Red, white, and blue bunting was draped from the windows of tall buildings. American flags were waving. The noise was deafening as we snaked our way down Main Street. It was hard for our large family to stay together. Three and a half-year-old Hans escaped a few times, but we managed to snatch him back.

Above: M. E. Church from Locust Street, Below: Thomas' Store, Main Street, Johnstown, PA. Both photos taken after the flood, May 31, 1889, Johnstown, PA.

After a parade of marching bands with shiny brass instruments, Papa guided us to Central Park. At the park, Papa paused in front of a polished granite bust that looked something like the face of George Washington.

"It's Mrs. Barend!" exclaimed Hans.

This response prompted a series of chortles from my teenage brothers. Actually, the firmly set jaw and stern features did resemble Mrs. Barend, our next-door-neighbor.

"No, Hans. This is Joseph Johns, the founder of Johnstown. This statue was commissioned by the German-American Alliance of Pennsylvania," Papa said proudly.

Papa himself had come from Germany in 1892. Papa found work in the coal mines; and shortly after, he arranged for Mama, Gertie, and Otto to join him in America.

Papa could do so much well...except play the organ. He even built our house. The story goes that when it came time to build, Papa let Mama select the location. They went all over town to find just the right spot. They looked on Westmont Hill and even downtown. Mama wanted to live on a hill...maybe because of the flood stories. When they went to Prospect Hill, Mama fell in love. It was just what she wanted.

Papa designed the house with Mama's input. Mama wanted lots and lots of windows.

"I don't know, Caroline," Papa said shaking his head. "Windows make a house harder to build. And windows cost a lot of money."

"Please, Jacob," Mama pleaded. "I want a lot of light to stream into our home. I want to be able to look out at all the trees and enjoy this beautiful hillside."

The house at 413 Prosser Street was built with many windows.

The story continues that after the house was built, Mama wanted blinds for the windows.

"Now you want blinds?" Papa asked shaking his head. "I thought you wanted a lot of light? I don't know, Caroline. Blinds cost a lot of money."

Broad Street, Johnstown, PA

Blinds were installed on each window...and later lacy curtains...and later lush draperies. Mama had good taste.

Mama wasn't like the other German ladies I knew in our neighborhood. She didn't clomp around like Mrs. Barend. Mama wore high heels and a feathered hat when she went into town, and she never clomped. I thought she was beautiful. She was tall and slim. Her hair was held up with celluloid combs, but curly wisps framed her face and trailed along the nape of her neck. I loved the beautiful aprons she donned for Sundays. I watched in fascination as she reached her hands behind her waist to tie bows that were works of art.

As far as the children go, first there was Gertie. Then there was a series of five boys: Otto, Fritz, Max, Ted, and Rudi. Charlotte and I followed all those boys. And then came Hans.

Mama loved all her children, but she had a special relationship with Gertie. And, I believe she really loved Charlotte and me.

Charlotte had the nickname of Lottie, and she and I were inseparable. Lottie was the dearest and the best. I think Mama thought so too. After five tough boys at last she had a fair-faced little girl with shiny brunette hair. Lottie was naturally wise. She was talented too. She could thread a needle and sew a doll's dress at the age of four.

9

I acquired a nickname too. My oldest brother Otto went off to Korea to work for awhile. He must have found a good job because he sent us such treasures that you would not believe. Otto sent my mother silks and laces. And he sent Lottie and me porcelain dolls, a brunette one for Lottie and a blond one for me. Gertie said the doll looked like me, and she called me *Doll*. The name stuck.

Our house had an upstairs kitchen and dining room, but we only used those rooms for special occasions. For everyday cooking, we used the basement kitchen. That was the domain of the females. There was a big black iron stove with filigree around the legs and four plates on top. We had to use a special tool to lift the plates to add coal. I polished that stove every Friday. Next to the stove was a scuttle full of lumps of coal. Cut wood and newspapers for the stove were piled in a corner. A sturdy table and benches made by my father sat on a large oval, braided rug. The benches were made special. The seats could be raised to reveal storage spaces. Papa kept some of his tools in these benches. There was a peacock blue hammock hanging in the corner where we often tried to lull Hans into napping. However, Hans preferred to explore the contents of the benches.

One day Mama discovered Hans pounding nails into one of the benches using a hammer and nails he found inside.

"Jacob, look what your son is doing! Stop him," demanded Mama.

"Oh, let him go, Caroline. He is learning. He will become a great woodsman," assured Papa.

"He is learning to be spoiled," warned Mama.

Mama was a gifted seamstress, gardener, and cook. She taught Lottie and me her secrets. We shredded cabbage and made sauerkraut that was stored in fifty pound barrels. A heavy lid was placed on top of each barrel, and a heavy brick had to be placed on top of the heavy lid to keep the sauerkraut under control. There were also barrels of pickles, bins of potatoes, and casks of apples which were stored in the back cellar. We canned tomatoes, pears, peaches, and plums. We cooked up jars and jars of jellies and preserves. There was a storage pantry lined with shelves. All the sweet treats, such as the pears, cherries, and peaches, were stored on the highest shelves, away from little hands, meaning little Hans. The sweet fruits were saved special for Sundays.

Lottie and I worked hard helping Mama, and I guess the boys were working hard too. So Mama would buy us something special. Every Saturday Herman Beerman would come by in his flat-topped wagon selling fruit. Every Saturday night after our baths, we each got an orange and a banana before going to bed.

Shortly after the Great Flood Memorial there was a knock on the front door. A telegraph was delivered for Gertie from her husband. The message read that Gertie's husband urgently wanted her back home in Canada.

"Oh, what shall I do?" exclaimed a flustered Gertie.

"Your husband needs you home. You should go as quickly as possible," said Mama. "You hurry down the hill into town. Go to the train station and reserve your ticket. I will get Helen ready, and I'll follow along with Helen in a short while."

So that is what happened. There were hurried kisses and good-byes, and Gertie was gone. Mama readied Helen and took the baby down to the train station. It was all very rushed. Mama didn't want us to go with her as she thought too many trailing along would slow her down. Time was of the essence as Gertie could catch the 4:00 p.m. train if all went well.

Mama saw Gertie and Helen off on the train. Then Mama started the long climb back up Prospect Hill. A neighbor found her collapsed on the road, and Mama was rushed as quickly as possible to Conemaugh Memorial Hospital.

When we got word that Mama was in the hospital, Lottie and I were naturally alarmed. Papa rushed to the hospital which was located clear on the other side of the city. Back in those days, it was not very easy to travel that far; but Mr. Lipka took Papa on his horse.

"You girls stay here, look after Hans, and cook dinner for your brothers," Papa commanded.

We spent an anxious evening waiting for news. Papa returned after dark and quietly announced that the baby Mama was carrying did not survive.

"But the doctor says that since your mother is so strong, she should live," Papa whispered with tears in his eyes. "She just needs rest."

Lottie and I hugged each other and Papa. I felt a mixture of relief and sadness.

Memorial Hospital and Nurses Home, Johnstown, Pa.

Memorial Hospital and Nurses Home, Johnstown, PA

Mama spent the next two days in the hospital. Lottie and I stayed home, watched Hans, and tried to keep the house going as best as we could.

Late on the third day, Max barged in and announced, "Mother is supposed to come home tomorrow!"

We rejoiced!

Lottie, who was always thoughtful, said, "We should give this house a fantastic cleaning so it will be spotless for Mama when she comes home."

We girls dug in and cleaned. We polished and shined. We dusted and swept. We threw the carpets over the clothesline and beat them with sticks. The next morning Lottie and I were on our hands and knees scrubbing the blue and white linoleum of the upstairs kitchen when we heard clomping across the wrap-around porch to our back door.

Lottie and I looked at each other. "Mrs. Barend," we simultaneously whispered.

Indeed, Mrs. Barend was at our rear door glaring in at us.

Lottie and I rose from our hands and knees and went to the door.

"How do you do, Mrs. Barend," said Lottie.

"What you mean, 'How you do?'" replied our next-door-neighbor in a thick German accent. "What you girls doing?" she continued, leaning forward with her left hand on her substantial waist and her right index finger pointing at us.

"We are scrubbing the floor," Lottie politely replied.

"What on earth for?" demanded Mrs. Barend.

"Our mother will be coming home today," I chimed in.

"Hmmph. Oh, your mother will be coming home today all right," said Mrs. Barend. "Your mother will be coming home today in a casket!"

And that is how Lottie and I learned that our mother had died.

Main Street East, Johnstown, PA

Chapter Two
1915

Mama's casket was brought home to 413 Prosser Street for her viewing. It was a misty day as her casket was placed into a horse-drawn carriage that had black fringe hanging from the roof. We followed the carriage through the valley and up another hill to Grandview Cemetery.

Although Papa was usually a man of few words, his eulogy lingered in our hearts.

"Dear Caroline was taken from us suddenly. The doctor tried to console us that she did not suffer. We are suffering. We are sick with grief. We are deep in sorrow. But God's will be done. And He does not want us to be troubled but to continue to live and rejoice knowing that beloved Caroline is resting in His glorious love. And I believe we can be certain that adored Caroline is now one of heaven's most special angels. She was beautiful...beautiful in life...beautiful in death."

The following weeks and months became something of a blur. We thought it was the end of the world. But, as God willed, we carried on. It was probably good that Lottie and I had so much to do. We were too busy to have much time to feel sorry for ourselves. Lottie and I cooked and cleaned continuously. But yet, there was a constant ache in our hearts: sometimes dull and in the background, sometimes sharp and wrenching.

My three oldest siblings were out of the house. Gertie was with her family in Canada. Otto was still away in Korea. And Fritz had married young. Fritz, his wife Millicent, and their baby Camilla lived in a nearby town. Still there were Max, Ted, Rudi, Hans, and Papa for Lottie and me to keep.

And some were easier to keep than others. Ted was always easy to please, but Rudi was especially demanding. Lottie and I scrubbed the laundry by hand using a washboard. Then we had to press the clothes using an iron heated by spitting, red-hot coals. Rudi insisted that even his handkerchiefs be pressed a particular way. Not only the white cotton handkerchiefs but even the red and blue bandanna kind had to be ironed to a precise four points.

I remember rising early in the morning to a freezing house. Lottie and I brought in wood from the woodshed and coal from the coal shed. We put newspapers under the lids of the coal stove and then we laid the wood on top. That was followed by the lumps of coal. On the side of the stove was a long box for matches which we called a lucifer. Papa made it, and it contained long match sticks. After igniting a match, the newspaper and wood would catch fire; and then the coal would start to get hot. When the plates warmed, we put on water for coffee.

We carried out the coal ashes and emptied the pan of water from under the ice box. I usually ended up spilling the ashes and water.

After we washed the clothes, we hung them outside on the clothesline to dry. Then I used the leftover laundry water to scrub the porch, the walkways, and the necessary house.

The necessary house, or outhouse, was located way back of the house. Papa built it, of course. It was a two-seater. One seat opening was oval shaped, the size of a big meat platter. Then there was a lower seat to accommodate little people. That place had to be scrubbed with hot, hot soapy water a few times each week. That was my job. Papa framed this place of convenience with homemade trellises in an attempt to beautify it.

"Let's plant morning glories along the trellises," I suggested.

"How about roses?" added Lottie.

"No girls. I think we will plant grapes on the trellises," Papa said decisively. "Then we can made jelly...and wine."

Papa was always practical. I never ate the grapes which grew there.

Papa tried to keep us happy. After supper, Papa would gather us around and read to us from the *Bible*. He was a great storyteller, and sometimes Papa would relate German folk tales. But Papa's favorite thing to do was to play the organ. I wish I could say it was our favorite thing as well. Papa only played the organ on Sundays, after church and dinner. The organ was very ornate and sat in a corner of the parlor. I thought the instrument seemed to shrink into the corner trying to hide on Sunday afternoons.

Our parlor was lovely. We really only went in there on Sundays and on special occasions. Since it was the room where Mama's casket had been, I had a hard time going in there for quite awhile.

The organ was placed against a wall which was covered with wallpaper holding a vineyard of purple grapes with dark green leaves. A border of gold hugged the wall next to the ceiling. Portraits of my grandparents stared at us from elaborate gold frames. A hanging lamp with a stained-glass shade as well as small lamps on either side of the organ gleamed for us. The furniture in the parlor was something special. It was purchased for Gertie's wedding for the comfort of our visitors. There was a Chesterfield sofa in luscious green velvet. It was tufted with a large button in the center of each back cushion. A matching chair in the rich emerald material kept the sofa company. Two mahogany side chairs with graceful curves alluringly invited us to repose. A library table commanded attention at the center of the room. A rug decorated with dark pink roses rested underneath it all.

Off the parlor was the rarely-used formal dining room. On a homespun runner carpet was a walnut table topped with a lace tablecloth. Two crystal candleholders and a crystal bowl sat on the table. Whereas the parlor was rather dark because it only had one window, the dining room was quite bright, having two large windows. An oval mirror hung on a wall, and an ornate heating stove also made its home in this room. The most striking feature of the dining room was the immense china cupboard. Inside was a garden of treasures: plates with ivy, saucers with roses, and a teapot with violets. There was a dish for everything. My favorite items were the minuscule butter pats. Each butter pat was a small ivory square the size of a pocket watch on which we placed a small portion of homemade butter. But we only used them for holidays.

The stairs and a small hallway lay between the dining room and kitchen. This upstairs kitchen was an enormous, sunny room. The three windows were positioned to catch light throughout the day. The kitchen floor was laid with blue and white squares of inlaid linoleum. There was a black coal stove and a big farm table. Cupboards were built into the far wall. This room's most prominent feature was the coo-coo clock on the wall that our parents brought from Germany. The clock was of dark wood. Small trees and woodland creatures were carved into its exterior. On the hour, a little boy and girl holding hands popped out of a tiny door.

Three bedrooms laid upstairs. The room above the dining room was for Papa. The room above the parlor was shared by Lottie and me. The biggest room, directly above the kitchen, was for all of the boys. Those rooms were frigid during the winter. Lottie and I huddled under our quilts, glad to have each other for warmth.

Behind our house was a good-sized piece of land. That was where we planted our vegetable and flower gardens, but there was still plenty of space for running and playing. A swing was roped from a weeping willow tree. In addition to the outhouse, there was a barn which housed our cow named Star. There was a hayloft where pigeons, and other visitors, nested. We kept chickens and ducks. The boys even made a manmade pond where the ducks could swim.

Papa saw how hard all of us were working, and he tried to fill the void Mama left behind. Rarely did we venture off Prospect Hill; but the summer after Mama passed on, Papa treated us to a few excursions. Our favorite jaunt was riding the trolley across town to Luna Park. There was something there for everyone. Papa and Ted liked the half-mile racetrack. Lottie and I enjoyed looking at the racehorses in their stables. Max and Rudi preferred to join in the baseball games. And Hans loved all the excitement.

There was a lake for rowboats. Young men slid oars into the water as fashionable young ladies with parasols perched on their shoulders sat taking in the day. Music bellowed from a dance hall, although Lottie and I were too young to enter.

The most amazing section of Luna Park was the carnival area. A Ferris wheel loomed into the sky. Passengers wobbled precariously in little metal carts stuck on spokes. Something called a roller coaster snaked close by. Awful screams came from its carts. These rides looked terrifying to me, although I think I could have handled the carousel. Thankfully we did not have enough money to even consider riding these amusements. However, the brothers were wide-eyed.

Luna Park

Later that summer, Papa took us to a place called Ideal Park. This place had the most enormous swimming pool we had ever seen. I looked out in amazement at all the splashing bodies in the water. But the most spectacular sight was at the far end of the pool. There sat a Ferris wheel.

A worker, noticing my amazed expression, explained, "That there's our Water Wheel. Folks climb on board, go around in the air, and get dumped into the pool on their way down. You should try it."

"Oh no, I don't," I thought.

But the boys did, even Hans.

"He's too small!" cried Lottie.

"He can't even swim!" I reasoned.

"Oh, we'll hold him tight," assured Max. And off they went.

"Our mother would never have permitted this." Lottie was firm.

Hans did more than survive the Water Wheel. He loved it.

"This isn't good," I said. "Hans is learning to be reckless."

That autumn, Lottie and I returned to school. After school we cooked and cleaned...and cleaned and cooked. Thanksgiving without Mama was very hard. Even more difficult was Christmas.

According to German tradition, the mothers always decorated the evergreen tree on Christmas Eve. Then the children were greeted the next morning to a glorious sight. Papa, trying his best, suggested that this year we all decorate the tree together.

We strung garlands of popcorn and baked gingerbread figures to adorn the tree along with sparkly glass ornaments from the old country. Papa, who could do everything well but play the organ, made a little village out of wood to place under the tree. We tried to keep cheerful as Papa explained, as he did every Christmas, how the Christmas tree was brought to America by the Germans.

"The evergreen keeps its color all winter. It does not lose its leaves like the other trees. This special tree represents the Lord's promise of everlasting life," said Papa.

His words made us think of Mama even more.

My good cheer lasted until Christmas afternoon. The neighborhood kids were sliding down the hill past our house in brand new

sleds. I felt ashamed because I knew I was being babyish, but I burst into tears.

"Everyone's got a new sled but me," I wailed. I was really quite inconsolable.

I usually didn't cry, and I think I caught everyone off guard. Ted came to the rescue.

"Tell you what, Doll. I'll make you a sled," said Ted, giving me a hug. "And it will be better than any of those other sleds because it will be made just for you."

"When will you make it?" I asked, wiping my eyes with the backs of my hands.

Ted replied, "First thing tomorrow. There'll be no school."

I could not wait for the next morning. And Ted did not forget. I awakened to the sounds of hammering and sawing coming from the basement. I rushed down the steps to find Ted busy at work. My father had a treasure trove of tools and supplies from which to work. There were saws of all sizes, hammers from tiny to sledge, bolts, tacks, and nails. There were pieces of wood and pipe.

Ted had already cut out the piece for the seat and had drawn patterns for the runners. I watched him cut out the different parts. He arranged cross pieces on the two runners to hold the runners in place. He attached everything together, adding metal to the bottom of the wooden runners. He obtained the metal from pounding out two pipes. It was beginning to look like a sled!

"Is it almost ready?" I asked.

"Not yet." Ted was always patient.

"When will it be done?" I persisted.

"Well, I think we need to paint it," Ted said.

We looked at each other and together said, "Red!"

And yes, Papa even had red paint in his treasure trove. Ted carefully stroked the bright paint onto the new sled.

"When can I ride it?" I asked.

"Not yet," Ted said. "We'll need to let it dry real good...maybe two or three days."

My heart sank. Two or three days seemed like next Christmas to me. But two days later the sled looked even more beautiful.

"Now can I ride it?" I asked.

"Not quite yet," was Ted's answer. "We still need to do a few things."

Ted went to the laundry basket and cut off a length of clothesline.

"For the rope...to pull it!" I caught on.

"Right," said Ted as he threaded the rope through the holes he had bored in the wood and tied the ends with a tight knot.

"Now can I take it outside?" I pleaded.

"There's still one more thing," Ted said.

I was worried, and a lump was forming in my throat.

"Just wait and see," said Ted. He strode into the basement kitchen, picked up a poker, and stuck it into the burning coals. He returned to the sled with the iron rod that now had a glowing red tip.

Ted started branding something into the new paint of my beautiful red sled.

Now I was really worried, and tears started welling in my eyes. "What are you doing, Ted? Please don't ruin it!" I gasped.

Ted laughed and said, "You'll see. Don't worry."

I crept closer and saw that Ted had formed a perfect *D*. That first letter was followed by an *O* and then two *L*'s. He had personalized my sled. I gave him a big hug. And Ted was right; my sled was better than the other kids' sleds. Mine was made to fit me. Mine was bright red. Mine had my name engraved on it. And mine was made with love.

Papa saw how hard Lottie and I were trying. We'd go to school and then come home and work.

"This is no life for little girls," Papa cried. "Something must be done."

And after the holidays, something was done.

Chapter
Three
1916

Papa sat Lottie, Hans, and me down at the kitchen table.

"Gertie is on her way for you. The three of you will stay with her for awhile," Papa announced.

"All the way in Canada?" I asked.

"Yes," Papa said. "So you'd better start packing up your clothes, books, and small things you want to take with you. Be sure to pack your warmest clothes."

"Who will cook and clean here for the rest of you?" asked Lottie.

"Your cousin Minerva will be arriving later this week to be our housekeeper. Minerva is older and can handle the work. You young girls," Papa said shaking his head, "You young girls...it's too much for you...this house...and school...I'm sorry."

Our cousin Minerva was eighteen years old. We had met her just a few times before, but she was old enough to manage a household better than Lottie and I could.

"Do we get to ride a train?" piped up Hans excitedly.

Lottie and I looked at each other. I could read Lottie's look. Hans was the only one happy about this arrangement.

Lottie and I obediently, but sadly, packed our belongings and rode the train to Sudbury, Ontario, with Gertie and Hans. Gertie tried to be good to us, but she was a young bride with a family of her own to manage. The cold months we spent in Canada froze together, but one recollection stood out. Gertie liked to play matchmaker and was determined that our oldest brother, Otto, should marry Sophie, the daughter of the Queen's Hotel owner. Gertie and Sophie had become fast friends. Otto had visited Gertie in Canada on his way to Korea. Apparently, Gertie had arranged a meeting between Otto and Sophie which went very well.

"Sophie will be the perfect wife for Otto," Gertie said. "She is refined and intelligent, not to mention sweet and kind." Gertie clasped her hands under her chin with joy. "And, Sophie will be the perfect sister-in-law for me!"

Lottie, Hans, and I had been in Canada for a few months when Gertie received a letter from Otto. Gertie was giddy as she opened the letter.

"Otto is back from Korea!" Gertie enthused. "He's in Johnstown...at the family homestead."

Gertie grew silent as she read on. Her brow furrowed.

"What?...What?...No!...Oh my Lord, no!" Gertie cried as she crumpled up the letter and hurdled it into the blazing fireplace.

I had never seen Gertie in such a state. She stood up and paced with agitation. She stormed from the room, and a door was slammed. Soon we heard high-volumed voices.

"What is he doing?" That was Gertie. "He's making a huge mistake. What is he thinking?"

"Calm down, Gertie." That was Gertie's husband, Robert. "Are you sure?"

"Yes, I'm sure," yelled Gertie. "What a fool he is! Good heavens, Robert, they're cousins!"

"Are you positive you read the letter correctly?" asked her husband.

"Yes!!" screamed Gertie. Then she wailed, "Oh, what will I tell Sophie? She'll be absolutely devastated."

We heard Gertie's footsteps pacing anxiously across the hardwood floor, and then she burst out, "I'm sick and tired of trying to help my family. I try and try, and what good does it do?"

Our oldest brother Otto had returned to 413 Prosser Street after working in the Orient for a few years. And...he fell head-over-heels in love with Minerva. Gertie was so disappointed, angry, and disgusted with Otto that she decided she was fed up with the entire clan. Her anger carried over to us. Soon Lottie, Hans, and I found ourselves on a train. This time bound for Johnstown, Pennsylvania.

Hans was again excited to be riding a train. "Some day," the five-year-old promised, "I'm gonna ride a train clear over to California."

"I'm just so happy to be going home," said Lottie. "I love our house. It is where we belong."

"I can't wait to see the parlor and our bedroom...everything!" I added.

The tall, blond-haired, blue-eyed, cheerful figure of Otto greeted us at the train depot. We were so excited to see him. Otto must have been a mindreader because he gave a toy train to Hans. And then he presented Lottie and me with small boxes. We popped them open and gasped. In each box was a gold ring from the Orient. In the center of each ring three creamy pearls sat in a row. We hugged him tightly. Never did we have such treasures!

We raced up Prospect Hill to home. I threw my arms around Papa and Ted...and even Max and Rudi. Papa had tears in his eyes and a grin on his face. I knew we had been missed.

"I'm so sorry girls," Papa gushed, hugging us again. "I thought the arrangement would have been easier on you. I'm so sorry. It's so good to have you back."

Behind the males I spied a diminutive figure with mousy brown hair.

"Oh," Papa announced, suddenly realizing the figure was being left out. "You remember your cousin, Minerva."

"Yes, how do you do?" I said.

Lottie merely said, "Hello."

"Are you going to marry Otto?" asked Hans.

"Yes, indeed," beamed Otto, putting his arm across Minerva's shoulder. Minerva blushed. The contrast between tall, blond, handsome Otto and short, brunette, nondescript Minerva was noticeable.

"It's so good to be home," I squealed. "I want to run through each room!"

My enthusiasm was short-lived however. The house had changed in the months we were gone. The homestead showed signs of neglect for the kitchen floor was grimy, the shelves were dusty, and the corners were cobwebbed.

"Minerva will fix you a good meal," Otto boasted. "She's a great cook."

"At least she's good at something," Lottie whispered looking about.

Further disappointment hit us when Lottie and I reached our bedroom. Minerva had taken over our bed...and our dresser...and our closet.

"Great," said Lottie, setting down her satchel on a rug that looked as if it hadn't been shaken out since we left.

I was toying with the pearl ring Otto had given me. It slipped off my finger and bounced under the bed. As I knelt down to retrieve it, I shrieked, "Lottie, there's a whole family of dust bunnies under this bed!"

"I guess Minerva has had other things on her mind besides cleaning," said Lottie dryly.

"Like what?" I was still young.

"Like catching a husband," replied Lottie.

After a cozy night of the three of us females sleeping in one bed, we headed downstairs to start the day. As we were preparing breakfast, Max came in with a copy of *The Johnstown Tribune*. Soon the brothers were all abuzz over the main story. A trolley car of the Southern Cambria Railway had lost control and wrecked head on into another trolley. Twenty-six passengers lost their lives. The photograph on the front page showed a trolley car that resembled an accordion.

"We should go look at the crash site," suggested Rudi.

"We'll go after breakfast," said Max. "Who all is coming along?"

"Me!" said Hans.

"No!" said Lottie. "Why do you want to see such a horrible site? And Hans is too young to expose to such things. He'll have nightmares."

Lottie was outnumbered by the brothers; and Hans, who usually got his way, accompanied them.

"You coming, Minerva?" asked Otto.

"Oh sure!" chattered Minerva.

As soon as everyone left, Lottie let loose. "Can you believe it? This house is a disgrace! And our housekeeper is gadding about! I'm glad Mama isn't here to see this mess. It looks as if a trolley crashed into *this* house! Minerva...she has a lot of nerve."

Lottie was furious. Lottie, who was always the patient one. Lottie, who was always the calm voice of reason. But she was right. The house was in a sorry state.

"Well, at least we can dig in and do some cleaning while the others are gone. They won't be around to interfere," I said.

And dig in we did. The coal stove, which I used to polish every Friday, had layers upon layers of grease on it. There were crumbs all over the basement kitchen floor, and mice in the food pantries. We dusted, swept, and scrubbed.

The thrill seekers returned filled with vivid details.

"I hope I get to see lots of wrecks like that one!" expressed Hans. I worried.

Mr. McClusky had taken Otto under his belt. Mr. McClusky lived in the neighborhood and was an avid fan of boxing. Although all my brothers grew to be over six feet tall, Mr. McClusky saw something special in Otto and wanted to make him a boxer. Mama did not want Otto to be a pugilist. She felt that boxing was barbaric; and when Mama was alive, she forbid Otto from fighting.

When he returned from Korea, Otto started training with Mr. McClusky. Otto jogged and did push-ups. He did countless jumping jacks and squats. Unfortunately, a good section of the basement kitchen was converted into training headquarters. Mrs. McClusky would not allow a gym in her house. They even attached a punching bag to the basement ceiling. That meant that we girls had to start using the upstairs kitchen more.

Mr. McClusky promised Otto that great things would happen.

"You have the talent, my boy. And you have the size," he would say.

Otto was an eager protege; and of course, he received plenty of encouragement from the brothers.

"*Killed By Hatpin,*" Max read from The Johnstown Tribune. "*Coincidentally with the introduction of a bill in the Legislature regulating the length of hatpins, Captain Andrew Englund, a well-known navigator, is dead as the result of being jabbed in the cheek with a*

The Johnstown Tribune, *Trolley Accident*

long hatpin. The accident occurred when Englund was riding in a crowded trolley car. Blood poisoning set in, and the victim died in agony."

"Ahh! Ahh!" cried Rudi as he toppled to the floor holding a long matchstick to his cheek.

How about this one, said Rudi, scrambling back to his chair. *"Foreigner Blows Head Off With Dynamite."* It says here, *"Despondent, it is thought, because he had been refused further employment in the Shoemaker Coal Mining Company's mines...on account of fits to which he had been subject ever since he had his skull fractured by being hit over the head with an ax in a fight two years ago, Steve Zolnar, a foreigner about thirty years old, blew his head off with a stick of dynamite on the back porch of a foreign boarding house about 7:30 o'clock last evening. He put the dynamite in his mouth, lit the fuse, and calmly waited until the explosive ended his life. The man's head and part of his chest were blown away, his brains were scattered about for many feet, part of the hair and skin from his head was plastered against the side of the house, the body was tossed about*

Trolley car downtown Johnstown, PA

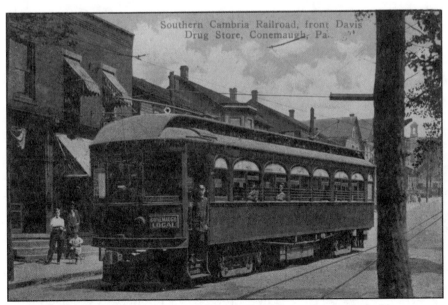

Southern Cambria Railroad in front of Davis Drug Store, Conemaugh, PA

Trolley crash.

fifteen feet, the lower part of the door on the house was blown in, and a hole almost three feet in diameter was knocked through the bottom of the porch...”

Thwack! Lottie hit Rudi over the head with the other rolled-up section of the newspaper. “That’s just awful! And Hans is right here listening to every word you say.”

Indeed, Hans was close at hand, soaking in every juicy detail. “That’s a great story,” said Hans. “Tell me more.”

“See! See what you’ve started!” chided Lottie.

“Oh, I’ve got a good story,” said Max.

“Tell me! Tell me!” begged Hans.

“Well, I don’t know if you’re old enough to handle it,” warned Max, folding up the newspaper.

“Sure I am,” asserted Hans.

Max shook his head, “I don’t know. It’s pretty scary.”

“Please Max. I can take it,” assured Hans.

“Well, okay,” said Max.

At this point, Lottie indignantly stormed out of the room.

“What do you know about coal mines, Hans?” asked Max.

“Well, Papa used to work in one before he got the job at the steel mill,” said Hans. “I don’t remember, but they say Papa used to come home from work pitch black from the coal.”

"That's right," said Rudi. "Mama wouldn't let him upstairs until he washed in the basement. Mama always had a tub of water waiting, and she'd scrub his back for him."

"Just like a baby," observed Hans.

"Papa always cleaned up well, but some of the other miners never really get completely clean. There is black around their fingernails," informed Rudi, holding up his fingers. "Look at Mr. Barend's nails sometime."

"What you might not know, Hans, is that coal mines are places of high danger," said Max. "The men go deep underground to get the coal, and sometimes terrible accidents occur. Do you know where the Inclined Plane is?"

Hans shook his head in affirmation. The Inclined Plane was a famous landmark in the area. Built after the Great Flood, it held two trolley-type cars on tracks that scaled the hillside. The Inclined Plane transported people from downtown to Westmont Hill and back. The plan was that if there was another flood, people could quickly escape to higher ground on the trolleys.

"Well, there used to be a coal mine under that hillside," continued Max. "They called it the Rolling Mill Mine. It was a very successful mine...until the accident. Back in 1902 there was a gas explosion in that mine, and the mine collapsed. Over one hundred miners died in that explosion."

"I never knew that!" exclaimed Hans.

"Oh, yes," said Max. "They buried the bodies of most of the miners. But some bodies were never found. They say that hillside is haunted. They say that at night the lost miners' spirits roam among the trees looking for their friends, trying to save them. Some say that on the darkest nights, you can even see their lanterns flickering."

Hans gasped. "Max...have you ever seen the ghosts?"

"Well," said Max, "your big sister doesn't want me to scare you...so now's a good place to stop."

Hans's eyes were saucers.

A simple wedding service was planned for Otto and Minerva. "Will they live here with us after they get married?" I wondered. Lottie just glared.

Inclined Plane

Although I certainly was doing my share of the work, my thirteen-year-old sister was really the one running the house. Minerva could cook pretty well. But she created more mess than food.

"Minerva is getting on my nerves." Lottie would frequently mutter under her breath.

Lottie was pretty quiet by nature. She usually didn't say anything that didn't need to be said. She was wise and patient and understood people. I knew my sister well so I could tell she was deeply troubled. I sensed that when Lottie decided to open up, it would be memorable.

Pound...pound-pound...pound...pound. The dishes were rattling in the cabinet. We had to take the coo-coo clock off the wall for fear it would get knocked down. Otto and Mr. McClusky were training in the basement using the punching bag.

"Otto must be getting stronger," I said, peeling potatoes. "His punches are shaking the house more."

"Our mother would never have permitted this," said Lottie. She was scrubbing the blue and white linoleum floor.

That floor was a source of great pride for Mama. All the neighbors had plain wooden floors in their kitchens. We were told that ours was the first linoleum floor in the neighborhood. Mama loved the blue and white tile. It did make the kitchen brighter.

All of the sudden I was startled from my potato-peeling reverie by a scream from Lottie.

"Look! Just look at this!" shouted Lottie, throwing her rag down in disgust.

I went over to where Lottie was scrubbing the floor and saw what she was so upset about. The tile had starting pulling apart.

We looked at each other and read each others' thoughts. The punching bag was attached to the basement ceiling directly beneath.

Otto's boxing career never really materialized. He fought in just a few matches before he got hurt. He took a hard punch to his right ear that never really healed right. They called it a cauliflower ear, and it was not the prettiest thing to look at.

City Park and Nathan's Dept. Store, Johnstown, Pa.

Central Park and Inclined Plane

It was late in the summer when it happened. Minerva had left the flour and sugar canisters open (again), and bugs got in.

"Minerva is on my last nerve!" exploded Lottie.

Lottie stormed to Papa.

"They've got to go! They must go! They don't take care of this house. They don't love this house like Mama did. They are ruining it. There's not enough room here for newlyweds. They're married now. They need their own place. They should be out on their own."

"But who will take care of the house and take care of the boys?" pleaded Papa.

"I will," declared Lottie.

"What about school?" asked Papa. "It is too much for you to run a house and go to school."

"I'm done with school, Papa," announced Lottie. "I just finished eighth grade. That's enough. Besides, I'm needed here. I'll take care of this house like Mama did."

And, she did.

Chapter
Four
1917

Papa had a good long talk with Otto and Minerva. Soon they were gone.

Little by little the house and grounds were starting to shape up. The first thing we did after the departure of Otto and Minerva was to take down that awful punching bag. Of course the boys wanted it to stay, but the girls won that battle after Papa realized the damage the bag was causing to the house.

Around this time six-year-old Hans devised a new hobby. He enjoyed leaving *presents* for Lottie and me inside the storage spaces of the benches our father had built. One morning we heard the muffled meows of our cat Melody and couldn't figure out where she was. We called high and low only to find Melody tucked away inside one of the benches.

"You mustn't put Melody in the bench ever again," Papa warned Hans.

"Are you going to send me away to the Christian Home?" Hans seemed genuinely afraid.

"Not this time," said Max.

Hans had developed a fear of being sent to the Christian Home, which was the town's orphanage. Our next-door-neighbor, Mrs. Barend, had planted that idea in Hans's head.

"Your papa sent you away before," she would inform Hans on a regular basis. "He send you away again if you be bad boy. But next time, you go to the Christian Home."

We started settling into a routine. Lottie was keeping house. Rudi, Hans, and I were going to school. Papa and the older boys were working at the Cambria Steel Company. They worked shifts around the clock.

Cambria Steel Company at night

Every Thursday was payday. Papa and the boys always wore their Sunday best when they collected their pays. Everyone did. It was a way to show respect to the company and appreciation for their jobs. A few times I accompanied Papa to pick up his pay. It was always a fascinating experience. A long line would form in front of the business office of the Cambria Steel Company. Soon there was a sea of men wearing dark suits and derby hats, many of the men looking as if they had been freshly scrubbed. Occasionally there would be women in the crowd.

Papa would whisper, "Those ladies are here to collect their husbands' pays."

"Why?" I asked.

"Because those ladies don't trust their husbands," informed Papa, looking across the street at one of the many taverns of the city.

One day after school, my friend, Marjorie Teschonek, teased me. "Doll, if you come home with me, I'll give you a surprise."

Intrigued, I walked home with Marjorie. She took me down to her family's basement kitchen and over to shelves stocked with supplies.

Moving a stool into position, Marjorie smiled, "I am going to give you a taste of something wonderful!" She climbed upon the stool to reach the top shelf. Marjorie slowly reached for a heavy paper carrier with wire handles. Slowly, she descended from her perch, carrying the small box as if it would break. Carefully Marjorie placed the package on a table and reached for a spoon. As she lifted the flaps of the container, an unusual smell emerged.

"What is it?" I asked.

"Just wait and see!" ordered Marjorie as she inserted the spoon and drew out a dark beige glob.

"It resembles ice cream, but it can't be," I said, realizing ice cream wouldn't be stored on a pantry shelf.

"You're right. It's not ice cream, but you must try it. It came from Coldrens," Marjorie explained.

Coldrens was an exclusive store that sold only the best and freshest in vegetables, meats, fish, and even flowers. My family didn't often shop there, just on the most special of occasions.

I hesitated. I wasn't sure of the blob that looked like ice cream but wasn't.

"Come on, Doll," encouraged Marjorie. "You'll love it!"

"Are you sure it's safe?" I asked.

"Oh, please!" Marjorie sounded a little irritated. "Just open your mouth!"

I closed my eyes and opened my mouth. Marjorie put the spoon in my mouth...and I had my very first taste of peanut butter!

As 1917 wore on, there was more and more talk of war. There was a war raging in Europe, and it looked like the United States was close to becoming involved. German submarines were attacking ships containing innocent passengers. And the Germans apparently tried to provoke Mexico and Japan into attacking the United States.

On April 6, Congress officially declared war. President Wilson said our involvement in the war was...*a crusade to make the world safe for democracy.*

Papa often sat over the newspaper looking sad and lost in thought.

Papa continued to try to entertain us by reading to us, telling us stories, and playing the organ.

"I can't believe not one of my children wants to learn how to play the organ!" Papa sounded hurt. "I will teach you. It is such a beautiful instrument. Johann Sebastian Bach, who was German, composed magnificent music for the organ."

"Too bad Papa can't play any of it," whispered Rudi.

I pinched Rudi's arm for his rudeness, but really Rudi had a point. On Sunday afternoons Papa would go into the parlor and head toward the organ. It actually seemed as if the grapes on the parlor wallpaper shriveled up as he played.

Papa was better at telling stories. One story that caused controversy in our household was the story of Morley's dog. Morley's dog was a statue of a German shepherd that was located in a downtown park across from City Hall.

"That was a very special dog," Papa would explain. "That German shepherd was owned by a man named Mr. Morley. James Morley, who was a good man, managed the Cambria Iron Mines. It's been told that during the Great Flood that dog pulled people, including Mr. Morley and several small children, from the raging waters to safety."

"That's hogwash," Max would argue. "That statue was just a lawn ornament that got washed across town in the flood."

Morley's Dog

It happened in early summer. The notice came. Ted had been drafted into the service. He would be leaving soon, within a week. He would be shipped overseas, probably to France.

Papa cried. Max and Rudi quit joking. Lottie was silent. I was gripped with anxiety. Once again, Hans saw the events differently.

"Wow! Ted, you get to wear a uniform and shoot a gun...Pow! Pow-pow!" said Hans, pantomiming his use of artillery. Rudi quickly escorted Hans away.

"How are you feeling about this, Ted?" asked Lottie.

"Well, I'd rather stay here with all of you," Ted smiled. "But I've got to serve my country."

That was Ted, always noble and ready to help others.

That week Lottie and I laundered and pressed Ted's clothes before neatly packing them away in a satchel. We prepared Ted's favorite meals, which wasn't hard because Ted liked everything. A strange feeling of solemnity hung throughout the house. When I passed by Ted, he would pat my hand or kiss the top of my head.

Finally the day arrived for Ted's departure. He dressed with care in his best clothes. He even wore the cufflinks Mama had given him for his Confirmation. The cufflinks bore the initials *TWE*, for Theodore Wilhelm Edelweiss. He looked very handsome.

We all dressed in our best for the slow walk down Prospect Hill to the train depot downtown. The station was packed with other young men and their families. There were plenty of American flags. Mothers and fathers gripped their sons. Some were silent. Some wept and wailed. None were happy.

The train pulled up to the platform with a hiss of gray smoke, and the young men started to board. The draftees were piled into a boxcar that had no seats. They had to stand.

"Like cattle!" sneered a tear-faced woman.

Ted hugged us all and walked to the train. He turned and waved to us and even graced us with a slight smile before the boxcar consumed him.

That was when it hit me. This was the best brother. Ted showed respect to my father and to everyone. Ted was the one I could always trust. Unlike Max and Rudi, he never made fun of me or teased me. Unlike Otto, Ted was sensible and practical. Every payday, Ted gave all of his money to my father for the family. Ted was always patient with me when I burnt the potatoes or broke a dish. When I was sad during the first Christmas after Mama's death, it was Ted who built me my red sled with *DOLL* inscribed on it. This was the best brother. And I realized I might never see him again.

Penn Station

Chapter
Five
1918

"My son! My son!...Oh, my son!"

It was still dark as I opened my eyes. Lottie stirred beside me.

"It's Papa," muttered Lottie. "He's having another nightmare." She fluffed her pillow and rolled over.

Since Ted had left, Papa had been having terrible nightmares. I slipped out of bed and peeked in on him. He was quietly sleeping, but his bed covers were all in a tangle indicating the torment he must have endured.

The next morning Papa came to breakfast looking exhausted with dark circles under his eyes. The boys didn't notice. They were absorbed with the latest headlines. Yet another fire had hit the downtown area during the night. Fires were nothing new in Johnstown. We seemed to be plagued by them. Back in 1905, the Penn Traffic Company burned down. Penn Traffic was the biggest and best store in Johnstown. Ladies took the train from Pittsburgh to shop there. The store even had a ladies' sitting room where women could rest from shopping while waiting for their trains. Fortunately, Penn Traffic was rebuilt.

But this latest fire was even worse. Reports were that nearly an entire city block had been ravaged by flames. Of course, the brothers had to go downtown and be in on the thrill. And of course, they were excited when they returned sharing the details of the smoldering buildings. A church had even collapsed in the disaster.

In order to calm everyone down, especially Hans, Papa read one of his favorite stories to us. It was a German folk tale called *King of Magic, Man of Glass*. Even though I knew the story backwards and forwards, I enjoyed my father's reading of it. In the story, a young man lives with his loving mother. They lead simple lives but have everything they really need. The young man is unhappy and wants more. He doesn't appreciate what he has. He doesn't value his mother's love. He doesn't see the beauty of the Black Forest which surrounds him. He goes to his magical godfather and asks for money. The godfather gives the young man money which he quickly spends. The young man returns and demands more money from the godfather. The magical godfather again gives the young man money. The pattern of the godfather giving the youth money continues. The young man is content for a short while but always becomes forlorn. He travels the world and is still miserable. He finally realizes that what he most needed he had back at home all along. He saw that the Black Forest was more beautiful than the faraway lands where he had traveled. And back home he had the love of his family.

Papa read to us a lot, especially from the *Bible*. We prayed a lot for the soldiers too, especially Ted. I thought about Ted every day. We didn't know much about Ted other than he was in France in deep trenches that were dug in the land. I tried to imagine what his life was like.

During this time Otto visited. I was glad to see my oldest brother. He looked good...except for the ear. His blondness and laughter lightened up our house. Otto had a carefree attitude that was a bit contagious. He never really seemed to worry too much. But Lottie did.

One day Lottie and I were shelling peas in the basement kitchen when she sat me down on one of Papa's benches.

"Do you know why Otto came?" she asked.

"To see us?" I suggested.

"Right," Lottie snorted. "He came to ask Papa for money."

"Why?" I asked. "I thought he was working as a carpenter."

"Well, you know Otto. Never wants to stay in one place for long. Remember how he ran off to Korea for adventure and fortune?"

"I don't think his fortune lasted," I supplied. "What does he want money for?"

During our talk, I felt movement beneath me. Absently, I assumed it was Melody rubbing against the bench.

"I didn't mean to eavesdrop...well, actually I did...but, anyway, I overheard Otto say he wants to go into the trucking business," reported Lottie.

"Trucking?" I asked.

"Yes. Otto predicts that trucks will be the wave of the future and that he can make a good business transporting things in them."

"Does Otto even know how to drive?" I asked. Cars and trucks were relatively new at the time.

"Oh, Otto thinks he can do anything," was Lottie's response. "He wants Papa to give him money to buy a truck."

"Papa doesn't have that kind of money," I said, now distracted by the movement of the bench.

I glanced behind the bench and didn't see our cat.

"Lottie, something strange is going on here," I said, rising from the bench and looking all around it. "This bench seems to be vibrating."

She came over and undauntedly lifted the lid. We jumped back.

"Oh my gosh!" I gushed.

"Quick," Lottie commanded. "Open the cellar door."

I ran and held the basement door ajar while Lottie tipped the bench over. A tiny skunk, that was really just a baby, spilled out of the bench and scampered out of the door. I quickly slammed the door and even locked it, which was something we never did.

Lottie and I breathlessly looked at each other. "Hans," we said in unison.

"Hans Herman Edelweiss, get down here this instant!" bellowed Lottie.

Hans soon slunk around the corner. "Yeah?" he said.

"Why did you do it?" interrogated Lottie.

"Do what?" asked Hans.

"Oh, come on," said Lottie as her face turned red. "You put that skunk inside the bench. Papa told you to never do that."

"No, he didn't," said Hans.

"Yes, he did," held Lottie.

"You're wrong. Papa said I should never put Melody inside the bench again. And I never have," defended Hans.

"A skunk. A cat. They're the same!" exploded Lottie.

"Actually, a skunk and a cat are two very different animals," reasoned Hans.

"Hans, why did you put the skunk in the bench?" I broke in.

"I found it while I was out playing. It came right over to me when I put my hand out. It was so cute that I wanted to keep it," he said.

We then tried to educate Hans about playing with wild animals and bringing them into the house. Hans required much instruction.

Otto stayed on a while longer. He and Papa had talks well into the night. Finally I learned that Papa had agreed to give what little savings he had to Otto. Otto went away but quickly returned. The expenses of the truck were far greater than he had anticipated. He asked Papa for more money.

"I guess Papa never read *King of Magic, Man of Glass* to Otto," mused Lottie.

This time we learned that Papa had used the house as collateral to get money to buy a truck for Otto. I really didn't understand what that meant.

"Papa, why are you doing this?" asked Lottie.

"Don't worry, Lottie," Papa said. "Otto can get his truck and become a successful businessman. And Otto has agreed to make the truck payments. It will all work out just fine."

"But why take such a risk?" pushed Lottie.

Pausing, Papa said tiredly, "One of my sons has gone away, and I may never see him again. If I can do something to help another of my sons, I must."

"MY SON!!! MY SON!!! MY SON!!!"

I woke with a start. It was very early on a Sunday morning. A pink dawn was just filtering through the lacy bedroom curtains.

"MY SON!! MY SON!! MY SON!!"

"Papa must be having an especially bad dream," I whispered to Lottie.

"OH, MY SON!! OH!! OH!! MY SON!!"

"Wow, his nightmares have never been this intense before," said Lottie, now wide awake. "Papa has too many worries."

"OH!! OH, MY!! OH, MY SON!!"

"Let's go check on him," I said.

We slipped out of bed and put our feet onto the cool floor. Not wanting to startle Papa, we gingerly opened our bedroom door and entered the hallway. Then we looked in Papa's room. We gasped.

A tall figure in a soldier's uniform was draped over our father's bed. The uniformed figure and Papa were embracing and sobbing. Ted had come home.

Communication was not very good at the time so we had no idea when Ted was coming home...or even if he was coming home. He had arrived on the night train and climbed Prospect Hill in the dark. Ted just walked right into the house. We never locked the doors, except to keep out baby skunks.

The day Ted returned was the happiest day of my life. Ted didn't talk much except to say that he was in France under General Pershing. He never complained about what he went through; but he kept repeating, "I'm so happy to be home. So happy to be here." He gave Lottie and me each one of his cufflinks that he wore when he left. The ones with *TWE* engraved on them. We later had them made into lockets so Ted would always remain close to our hearts.

The most magnificent parade Johnstown ever had was held in honor of the end of the Great War. I had never seen downtown so crowded or so decorated. The city was awash in red, white, and blue. We marveled at the patriotic bunting that was draped from the tallest buildings. We had no idea how the flags and bunting were installed at such high elevations, from five and six stories! We sandwiched our way between the crowds on the sidewalks. But people were of good cheer and didn't seem to mind being pushed about. Everyone was thankful the war was over and our boys were home.

The parade started with a cavalcade. The first horseman carried a massive American flag. The bugle, snare drum, and piccolos of the Keystone Band playing Revolutionary War tunes followed. Then came the brassier sound of the Citizen's Band. School children romped down the street waving flags and carrying *VICTORY BOYS AND GIRLS* signs. Legions of steelworkers proudly marched across the Franklin Street Bridge holding signs that read, *WE ROLLED THE BULLETS THAT LICKED THE KAISER* and *WE ROLLED 1,000,000 TONS.*

Then the crowd broke into a deafening roar. The doughboys were approaching. Confetti was flying. Whistles were blowing. People were laughing and shouting. The soldiers were getting closer and closer. Finally they were passing right in front of our eyes.

They marched in straight rows holding their heads up high. The crowd went even wilder.

"Do you think we'll be able to spot Ted?" I asked Lottie.

"I sure hope so," she shouted.

I didn't think it was possible. Not in that crowd. It was Hans, who was perched on Max's tall shoulders, who screamed, "There he is!"

At Hans's words, Ted turned his head in our direction, smiled, and saluted. How good it was to have him back.

Chapter
Six
1919

There were a few job changes after Ted returned from the war. Ted, who was always interested in electricity, trained to be an electrician. Max decided to leave the steel mill and learn the construction trade. Rudi started working at the mill, vowing to move out West as soon as he could. And, of course, Otto got his truck.

Papa continued working at the steel mill, and the business was strong. All kinds of contracts were pouring into the mill. An exclusive agreement was even made to manufacture all sled runners for Flexible Flyers sleds. In honor of the contract, the latest model of a Flexible Flyers sled was on display in front of Mueller's Store.

Rudi was antsy to spread his wings, but Lottie and I actually were not looking forward to his moving out.

"He's the only one Hans listens to," Lottie would say, speaking of Rudi.

It was true. Rudi was particular, opinionated, and vain; but he could keep Hans in line.

One frosty Saturday in January, Hans crashed through the door.

"What happened to you, child?" Lottie cried.

Hans's face was scarlet. His jacket and pants were splattered with blood. It was the worse site I had seen since Otto's final boxing match.

"I lost control of the sled and hit a tree!" Hans wailed.

"Oh, you poor dear!" I soothed.

Lottie and I cleaned Hans's wounds, which thankfully were minor, and showered him with attention.

"Well, you always said you wanted to see lots of crashes," I said, recalling Hans's fascination with his first crash scene, the trolley wreck.

Later that evening over supper, Papa reported that the sled in front of Mueller's Store was missing.

"That takes a lot of nerve," said Max. "That sled was right in front of the place."

Papa shook his head, "I don't know what this world's coming to."

"Maybe the wind blew it away," offered a bandaged-up Hans, focusing on his bean soup.

"Maybe somebody stole it," asserted Rudi.

"Hans," said Ted. Hans jumped. "Let me see that sled you used today. I'll see if I can fix it."

"Naw, that's all right," said Hans, intent on his soup.

"Well, it must be as banged up as you are," continued Ted.

"It's okay," said a meek Hans.

"There are so many sleds around here. Which one did you use?" I asked.

"Just one that was layin' around," was Hans's reply.

"Around where?" asked Rudi.

"Oh...just layin' around," whispered Hans.

"Around where?" pressed Rudi.

"Just a few streets over that way," answered Hans, indicating the direction with his head.

"Hans, did you take the brand new Flexible Flyers sled that was in front of Mr. Mueller's store?" interrogated Rudi.

"I call it *borrowing* a sled," defended Hans.

Everyone else called it stealing a sled.

It was Rudi who marched Hans to Mueller's Store to beg forgiveness. Mainly because Mr. Mueller was friends with Papa, he was easy on Hans. For punishment, Hans had to sweep the store after school. Ted repaired the sled, and Rudi made Hans return it.

"Rette deine seele! Rette deine seele!" Mrs. Barend yelled at Hans from over the hedge.

"Papa, what does that mean?" asked Hans.

"*Rette deine seele* is German for *save your soul*, my boy," said Papa.

My older brothers were all tall and handsome. Ted didn't know that he was handsome. Otto didn't care that he was handsome. I wasn't really sure what Fritz thought since I saw so little of him. Max and Rudi were very well aware that they were handsome.

"Max and Rudi think awfully highly of themselves," Lottie would mutter when she was fed up with them.

This was about the time when Max started courting Gretel. Gretel lived with her family in the corner house at the top of Prosser Street. She had a large family too, but just about everyone did in those days. Gretel had just as many brothers as I did.

Almost every day as Max returned from work, he would stop at her place. Gretel was always available to come out for Max, and they would talk across the back fence. This went on for months. Lottie and I would watch them from our kitchen window. Max and Gretel would talk and laugh for a long time.

Clearly, Gretel was deeply smitten with our brother. Lottie would try not to roll her eyes when Gretel would gush, "Maximilian is one in a million!" But the fact was Lottie and I really liked Gretel. She was a pretty girl who knew how to cook, sew, and clean. We all thought Gretel would be a good match for Max. There were hints of marriage.

One evening, Max went with some of his friends to a dance hall. That's where Max laid eyes on Frieda, a fair-haired Swedish girl. They were married by spring.

Gretel was devastated. I felt terrible for her. I would walk a longer route to avoid going past her house.

That summer there was a Prospect picnic. The entire neighborhood came together for food and games. The day was bright, and a festive mood wafted through the air. I sat down on a bench and was surprised when Carl, one of Gretel's brothers, sat next to me. I felt awkward and embarrassed about what had transpired. I was mute. I couldn't think straight yet alone say anything intelligent to Carl. I was further surprised, even shocked, when Carl grabbed my left hand. I looked up at him, and a strange smile was on his face. All of the sudden Carl squeezed my hand quite hard. In fact, it hurt.

"Do you feel that, Doll?" asked Carl.

Feeling flustered and not wishing to appear weak, I managed to say, "Ah...no."

"You're just like your brothers," Carl sneered, flinging my hand away. "You don't feel anything."

Gretel was crushed. And so was my hand.

Behind our house was a wooden barn. That's where Star the cow lived, along with an assortment of chickens and ducks. A ladder led to a loft where hay was stacked. Pigeons and other critters roosted up there.

Hans and his buddies loved to play in the barn. They swung from ropes strung over the rafters. They played tic-tac-toe by tracing the X's and O's in the dirt floor with a stick. Up in the loft the boys played checkers and cards and, I strongly suspected, smoked corn silk.

The summer had been hot and dry. One warm evening Hans announced he and his cohorts were going to have a sleep-out in the barn. I remember Papa worked night shift. Lottie and I retired, feeling wiped out from the heat. In addition to cooking and cleaning, we labored in the garden that day. I think I fell asleep before my head hit the pillow.

I dreamt I was in a large tent in the middle of a desert. I was with some other girls, and we were wearing long, flowing robes. The flame from a glass lantern cast shadows on the sides of the tent. It was hot and dry...so hot. I was extremely thirsty. The air grew oppressive. I heard the gallop of a camel approaching outside the tent. There seemed to be some sort of commotion. Shouts entered my dreams, as Lottie shook me awake.

"Doll, Doll, wake up! Hurry!!" Lottie cried.

I was roused out of my slumber to hear shouts and crackling. And there was a putrid smell.

We ran down the steps.

"Outside!" screamed Ted.

We fled outside to see the barn in flames.

"The kids!" yelled Lottie. "Where are they?"

Huddled under the weeping willow tree were Hans and his buddies. I ran to them and hugged them. They were visibly upset. Even Hans was shedding tears, which was rare for him.

"The lantern...The candle," confessed two boys simultaneously.

Rudi and Ted were throwing buckets of water on the flames as a fire truck rolled down the street. The men rolled out their hose and flooded the barn. The flames died, but so did the barn. The walls caved in. The barn was burnt to the ground.

"Oh, where's Star?" I cried.

We searched about but could not find our cow in the dark.

The next morning Papa walked home from work. When he reached the homestead, he thought something was different. It had been a long night, and he was tired.

Mrs. Barend ran out of her house and cried, "See...see what your boy do! Your boy bad. My boys aren't bad like your boy!"

That's when Papa realized that there was no barn.

Papa burst into the house and up the steps. Lottie and I were awake, of course, but Hans was still asleep. Papa grabbed the leather strap he used to sharpen his blades and stormed into the boys' bedroom. Hans was sleeping peacefully, looking as if he didn't have a care in the world.

"What did you do?" Papa bellowed.

Hans awoke with a start. Papa was usually kind and gentle. I had never seen Papa so angry. I really thought Papa might kill him. As Papa raised the strap to strike Hans, I jumped in front of Hans and spread my hands wide.

"Please, please! Don't hit him! It was an accident!" I cried.

Papa froze. Deep lines creased his forehead. His eyes were ice. His jaw was set. Finally, his muscles relaxed, and he lowered the strap.

"For the love you have for your brother, I can't do it," he said. Papa threw down the strap and left.

It was a tense day at 413 Prosser Street. Lottie and I kept the household running. While we were washing up the dishes, we heard a sound that made us smile.

"Moooo. Moooo." Star, who had been frightened off and probably spent the day in the woods, had come home.

That fall I was fourteen and in high school. Back in those days, it was a privilege to go to high school. Most kids stopped attending school after the eighth grade. I was shy by nature so naturally I was petrified to go to the big high school downtown.

My classes included English, typing, shorthand, and bookkeeping. We were told that these classes would prepare us for "stenographic employment." Also in the curriculum were domestic science and gym. We had gym twice a week "to avoid rounded shoulders and laziness."

Basketball and dodge ball were fun, but what I remember most were the uniforms we had to wear...and how I got in trouble because of them. For gym class, each girl had to wear a white, long-sleeved middie blouse and black bloomers. The black sateen bloomers loosely covered the full thigh and were gathered with elastic just above the knee. I wore gym clothes that were passed down to me from the Lipka family.

"Young ladies," announced Miss Lawrence, "we will start practicing for our exhibition."

"Exhibition?" I wondered.

"At the end of each semester, a gym exhibition is held for the students to demonstrate exercises and gymnastics," Miss Lawrence enthusiastically informed. "Oh, and your grade will reflect your participation in this exciting event."

I was shy by nature so I naturally dreaded this exciting event. We practiced jumping jacks and forward rolls for weeks. Each gym class I looked around. I inspected what the other girls were wearing. Some girls had brand new bloomers. I looked at mine which had several patches on them. Some girls had tennis slippers. I had no special gym shoes.

As the weeks progressed, I decided I could not participate in the exhibition. So, on the evening of the exciting event, I simply did not go.

Shortly thereafter report cards were issued. I felt I was a good student and tried my best. I expected a report card my father would be proud of. I opened the card. It read

English A

Typing A

Shorthand B

Bookkeeping A

Domestic Science A

Physical Education D

D! I was shocked. Deep disappointment set in. I would not be in the All A and B Club!

I was shy by nature so naturally I was terrified to confront my teacher, but I did.

"Miss Lawrence, please. I don't understand. Why did I get a *D*? I try my best in class."

"Well, Crystal." (In high school, I was called Crystal.) "You failed to attend the exhibition," explained Miss Lawrence. "You did not honor your responsibility. And you did not provide an excuse for your absence. Were you ill?"

"Well...no."

"Then why didn't you attend?" quizzed the teacher.

"I...I only have patched-up, hand-me-down bloomers," I gushed. "And the other girls have such beautiful, new bloomers and tennis slippers. I...I couldn't ask my father for money because he works so hard, and he is rebuilding our barn which got burnt down...And my mother passed away...and..."

Miss Lawrence placed her hand on my shoulder and said, "Crystal, let's go see Principal Lewis."

I was shy by nature so naturally I thought I would die if I had to speak with the principal. But somehow I did. I lowered my eyes and related my story. I glanced up. Principal Lewis stared gravely at me through wire-rimmed spectacles. I was shivering, and my palms were clammy. Principal Lewis took my report card, scratched out the *D*, and wrote in a *B*. I made the All A and B Club.

Otto transported all kinds of goods in his truck: furniture, kegs, lumber, and foods. Otto visited a few times that year and took us for rides in his new truck. Minerva and Otto came for Christmas and gave us a generous supply of foods. There were boxes of oranges, apples, and other delicacies.

"You still paying on the truck, Otto?" Papa asked.

"Yes, Papa," Otto said.

Franklin Street, East

Chapter
Seven
1920

"She couldn't keep a house clean. Why am I not surprised she can't keep a truck clean either!" Lottie complained, stomping on a rather large black bug scurrying across the kitchen floor.

We came to learn that the crates and baskets of fruits and delicacies that Otto and Minerva gifted us with at Christmas contained a special hidden surprise...bugs. Roaches to be specific. Our new tenants settled into 413 Prosser Street with ease, seeming quite comfortable with their new accommodations. And those bugs spread everywhere: in the flour, in the drawers, in the cupboards. It was awful. I shattered a plate from Germany when one of those little monsters crawled onto my hand. I hadn't seen the creature because it had camouflaged itself with the foliage painted on the dish. Lottie and I were disgusted. Of course, Hans saw things differently. He enjoyed chasing our new guests.

And boy, were those bugs hard to get rid of. They were even more stubborn than Rudi. Lottie and I cleaned and cleaned. We swept. We stomped. We squashed. Still our guests remained.

"I hope Minerva and Otto never come back," Lottie muttered under her breath, smashing a roach with a broom.

Finally we decided to open the windows to freeze out the bugs. It was January in Pennsylvania. We were not happy. Finally the pests disappeared, but it seemed as if it took all winter.

We were just beginning to thaw out when a larger vermin arrived. Lottie and I were preparing supper when there was pounding
at the front door. We jumped and ran to answer it. A thin, little man
twitching a thin, little mustache was on our porch. He wore a dark
suit and carried a satchel. I had never seen him before.

"Hello, may I help you?" Lottie asked.

"Well...ah...yes. Is this the Edelweiss residence...413 Prosser
Street?" asked the mousy man.

"Yes, it is," Lottie replied.

"May I please speak with the head of the household?" inquired
the mouse man.

"My father and older brothers are all at work. I am in charge at
the moment." And she was.

"Oh...Oh, well, I am from the Dollar Bank." The little man
clawed through his bag and produced some papers. "Well," he chattered, "I have been sent to notify members of this address that your
property is being foreclosed."

"What does that mean?" I cried.

"Payments for a truck have not been made to our bank. This
house was used as collateral." The little man squinted at his papers
and said, "One Otto Stefan Edelweiss has been notified repeatedly
that payments to the bank are due. We have received no response
from him. This house and grounds will become the property of the
Dollar Bank if payment cannot be made within ninety days." With
that, the mouse man tacked a large sign on our house that read in
bold letters *FORECLOSED*.

A very serious look overtook Lottie's face. She was silent for a
long time. Finally, she said, "Sir, since we have ninety days to make
payment, that sign should not be on our house yet."

"Ninety days, Miss," replied the rodent man nervously. "I was
ordered to put up the sign. What you do after I leave is your business." With those words, he thrust some papers into Lottie's hand,
wrinkled up his nose, and left.

Lottie's eyes bore holes into the back of the man as he retreated
up the street. Of course, Mrs. Barend was out on her porch shaking
out her rugs while all of this transpired. As soon as the little rat turned
onto Moore Street and was out of sight, Lottie grabbed the

Dollar Bank

FORECLOSED sign and ripped it off the house.

"Oh, you can't do...you can't take down that sign!" shouted our dear neighbor, wagging her finger. "They'll come and get you..."

We escaped into the house and didn't hear the rest of Mrs. Barend's lecture.

"Old busybody," Lottie muttered. "Always sticking her nose in our business."

"Lottie, what are we going to do? Will we have to leave our house?" I was liking our home again after the roaches had all gone.

"We are going to save our house," Lottie said determinedly.

That night we all sat down to discuss the matter.

Papa kept shaking his head and muttering, "Otto told me he was making payments. I can't believe my son would betray me."

"Why are you surprised?" quipped Rudi. "Anyone who marries his cousin isn't the sharpest pick in the coal mine. Personally, I think he took one too many blows to the head during his boxing days."

Ted and Lottie were the voices of reason.

"Look everyone," said Ted. "We will save our house. I will take on a second job to earn more money."

"And I can take in laundry to do," suggested Lottie. "Maybe I can even sew and cook for money. I've seen notices in *The Johnstown Tribune* requesting such services."

"I'll ask about working extra shifts," muttered Rudi. "Although I think Otto is a fink," he added.

Papa, Ted, Rudi, and Lottie loved our house so much that they were willing to push themselves to save it. It got me thinking.

My friend, Katherine Carshun, worked at a confectionery eatery downtown. She would tell me all about her work and how much she liked it. Katherine was sixteen and I was only fifteen, but I wondered if I could work there.

"Katherine, do you think I could get a job after school where you work?" I timidly asked.

"I don't see why not," said Katherine. "You'll need to talk with the owner, Mr. Lindrokis. Here, I have a menu you can look at."

LINDROKIS'S ELITES
JOHNSTOWN'S QUALITY CANDY STORE
OUR OWN MAKE—FRESH EVERY HOUR
CANDIES, ICE CREAM, AND PASTRIES
DAINTY LUNCHES
FRESH CUT FLOWERS DAILY
158 MAIN STREET, JOHNSTOWN, PENNA.

The next day I went downtown by myself. I wandered up and down the streets, taking the longest possible route to Main Street. I walked by the windows of Glosser Brothers Department Store a half dozen times. I strolled at a very slow pace through Central Park and glanced at the statue of Joseph Johns. Finally I reached Main Street. I stood on the sidewalk across from Elites, immobile like a statue myself. I stared at the front of Elites. Happy customers bustled in and out.

Finally I crossed the street. I took a deep breath and heaved open the heavy glass door. The rich smells of chocolate and baking greeted me. It was a whole new world in there. I found myself in a

Elites Candy Store

large room with mirrored walls. A balcony hugged a side wall. Marble-topped tables with wrought iron legs and matching chairs filled this mezzanine as well as the lower main floor. Dark paneling completed the areas that were not mirrored. White tile lay upon the floor. Fans with large wings buzzed from the ceiling creating a cool sanctuary.

Opposite the front door was a counter that extended the full width of the room. One end was stocked with beautiful candies and pastries. The other end had a soda fountain. Stools with red leather tops were parked in front of this section.

I crept toward the counter. I was shy by nature so naturally I was terrified. My tongue was sandpaper. My fingers were ice. I had trouble focusing. I felt like I was in a dream.

"Hey, girl!" smiled a curly, black-haired youth with a Greek accent. He was putting a cherry on top of a sundae. "What can I get you?"

"A...a...a job," I managed.

"Well, you'll have to talk to my uncle. Come, come," he said, ushering me behind the counter into a small office.

A distinguished-looking man with dark hair graying around the temples was bent over a roll-top desk. I stood awkwardly, feeling terribly out of place. I was just about to turn and run out when Mr. Lindrokis himself looked up.

"What do you want?" he asked, not meanly.

"A job," I said, with more confidence this time.

"How old are you?" he asked.

"Fifteen," I answered.

"Where are you from?" he asked.

"Prospect," I said.

"Who is your father?" Mr. Lindrokis continued.

"Jacob Edelweiss," I answered.

"German?" he asked.

"Yes," was my reply.

"Good, I like Germans," he said.

"You still in school?" was the next question.

"Yes, but I could work after school and on weekends." I started to relax ever so slightly.

"You make good grades?" he asked.

"Mostly A's and a few B's," I said.

"You sound a hard-working girl," replied Mr. Lindrokis.

He studied me for a long time and said, "You are tall. You can reach the high shelves. You are hired."

The next step was to convince Papa into letting me work downtown.

"My baby girl! My baby girl cannot work downtown. You are too young!" declared Papa.

"I am not a baby. I am old enough to work," I asserted.

"What about school? Lottie stopped going to school. I don't want you to stop school too," cried Papa.

"I won't," I assured him. "It's been arranged. I will work on weekends and after school."

"Oh no! That store does not close until late. I don't want you walking from downtown in the dark. Bad people come out after dark...And you are just a girl," Papa continued.

That is when I waved the newspaper in his face.

The Johnstown Tribune, *August 18, 1920*

"Look!" I cried. "Did you read the newspaper today? Tennessee became the 36th state to ratify the Suffrage Amendment. Women can now vote. And look at this picture!"

On the front page of *The Johnstown Tribune* was a cartoon of a woman and a man shaking hands. The caption simply read, "*EQUALS*."

"Papa, I really want to work to help save our house. Please let me do this to help our family."

Papa hugged me and said, "You are a good girl."

We all worked hard. And, we saved our house.

First National Bank, Johnstown, PA

Chapter
Eight
1921

" *'Best Minds' of All Times Soon to Run World Through Spirit Control, Mediums Say.* That sounds like a good one," announced Rudi browsing through *The Johnstown Tribune*.

"This one sounds even better," said Hans, now ten years of age. "*Elevator Kills Altoona Priest.* It says here: *The Reverend Father Zachary Girulomi, assistant rector of Our Lady of Mount Carmel Catholic Church, was fatally injured here today when he was crushed by a descending elevator in the Altoona Trust Building.*"

It worried me how Hans was following in his brothers' footsteps by turning to the newspaper for morbid entertainment. Nobody was amused, however, when the headline read *Seven Persons Are Killed and Eight Hurt When Theater at Barnesboro Collapses; Many Victims Children.* The article further read *Motion Picture House Is Totally Wrecked; Foundation Caves in as Result of Excavation on Property Adjoining Grand Theater; Fatal Crash Comes Without Warning; Several Hours' Work to Extricate Victims; Few Persons in Audience Escape Injury.*

"Gee...maybe that could have happened to us," voiced Hans. "Rudi, we just saw a show yesterday."

Perhaps there were some morsels of awareness and conscience developing in Hans...maybe...possibly.

That year, Max and Frieda had a son, Milo. The baby was precious, and we got to visit with the new family every once in awhile.

"You know, Doll," said Lottie. "In small doses...and not too often...Max is okay."

"I know what you mean," I said. "The baby really is adorable. Maybe Max has matured since he got married."

"Maybe," replied Lottie.

Our relationship with Max continued to improve...after he moved from 413 Prosser Street.

That summer Lottie and I were outside hanging up laundry to dry when we heard a frightful scream.

"What's that!" I jumped.

"I have no idea." Lottie was wide-eyed.

The terrible roar pierced our ears again.

"It doesn't sound natural," analyzed Lottie.

"Whatever it is, it sounds like it's in pain," I managed.

We dropped the wrung-out shirts and ran to the far back edge of our property. The sound seemed to be emanating from that direction.

Our sizable yard and gardens extended a good distance behind our house. Then the land dropped off steeply. A dense forest grew below. When I was younger, sometimes Lottie and I went down there in search of berries, but we would get scratched up pretty badly. It was quite wild down there. Of course, Hans and his buddies loved to prowl around in those woods. Papa said there used to be coal mines down there and to be careful because some of the mines had collapsed and sinkholes dotted the area.

Sometimes in the evenings after the dinner dishes were washed and put away, I would walk to the edge of that cliff and look out. From that point, I could look down into the trees and up to see the tops of nearby hills. I admit that I especially loved going there on chilly, fall evenings. The crisp wind would howl through the trees. I would imagine witches brewing potions in the forest below...or ghosts of miners trapped in collapsed coal mines. The wind would whip my hair and chill my bones. I'd scare myself silly and then run as fast as I could back to the toasty house.

Cambria Theater

This was a bright summer day so I didn't fear witches. But what was that awful cry?

"Should we go down and check?" I asked.

"Certainly," came from Lottie, who was already descending.

The bellowing continued. We followed, pushing aside branches and wading through high weeds.

The shrieking intensified.

Suddenly, we found ourselves in mushy ground. It was mud but tackier.

"Ewww, what is this stuff?" asked Lottie.

"I don't know, but it's terrible to walk in," I said.

The squealing sounded very near now.

"Star!!!" we screamed together.

"Oh, poor baby! What happened to you?" I cried.

All we could see was part of Star. She had fallen into a sink-hole. Star looked at us pitifully. Her huge brown eyes seemed to say, "What happened? Where am I?"

"What should we do?" I asked.

"Let's pull her out!" commanded Lottie.

We tried to pull her out, but we didn't have enough leverage.

"Ropes. We need ropes to pull her out," assessed Lottie.

"We'll be right back, girl," we said to Star.

Then we scrambled up the thorny cliff. Lottie headed for the clothesline and started ripping it down.

"There's more rope in the benches. I'll go get it," I panted.

I ran into the basement and started flinging open the bench lids. Hammers...nails...leather...spools of thread...candles...newspapers...

"No, no, no," I said, rummaging through embroidery hoops.

Finally, "YES!!!" I found the bench holding ropes. Hurriedly I grabbed a big armful of rope...and screamed! And I screamed louder than Star. I didn't have time to deal with my surprise at the moment. I slammed down the bench lid and ran, gladly, back outside.

"What's the matter?" asked Lottie, already heading back to the cliff.

"Hans!" I spat.

Actually, it was probably a good thing that I felt so incredibly angry at my dear little brother. I think that energy fired my strength because we managed to free Star rather quickly. I felt a sense of accomplishment to rescue a fallen animal. I would not always be able to do so.

While we were trying to clean Star...and ourselves, Lottie asked, "What were you screaming about?"

"Under the pile of ropes I found a special surprise...baby snakes!" I shuttered.

"What kind?" asked Lottie.

"I didn't stay to examine them," I replied dryly.

Lottie, who wasn't afraid of much, boldly opened the bench lid.

"Garters," she assessed.

I managed to peak over the edge. Tiny, slender tubes that resembled blades of grass were squiggling all over the bottom of the recess.

We looked at each other and asked at the same time, "Where's the mother?"

When Hans finally moseyed in that day, I gave him a piece of my mind. Then Lottie gave him an even bigger piece of her mind...and she refused to feed him dinner...and breakfast the next morning. Furthermore, Hans professed ignorance as to the whereabouts of the mother snake.

Hans asked, "Papa, do you think the Christian Home has any openings?"

"Son," Papa replied, "I don't think they'd take you. It's a *Christian* home, my boy; and your behavior is anything but Christian."

For the rest of that summer we tip-toed about the house, always checking before sliding our feet under a table or reaching into closets or climbing into bed at night. We never did find the mother snake.

My time was increasingly being spent working at Lindrokis's Elites. Mr. Lindrokis was a Greek immigrant who started this business. He named his establishment Elites. Mr. Lindrokis intended the name to be pronounced *a leet*, meaning *the best* or *the top of the line*. However, Johnstowners called it *eee lights*, and that pronunciation stuck.

I started waitressing the lower, center tables. That's where all the inexperienced waitresses began. The elevated tables on the mezzanine were reserved for the waitresses who were elite.

I worried about dropping since I had been known to drop a dish or two at home. But I tried to be extra careful and initially managed to avoid major mishaps.

The other waitresses were girls from Johnstown. The men who worked there were from Greece. Mr. Lindrokis owned and managed the business. His brother Nick helped him run the place. The cooks, dishwashers, soda jerks, and candy maker were all Greek; most of them were related to Mr. Lindrokis.

The candy especially intrigued me. Behind the glass display cabinet sat trays and trays of creamy brown candies in fluted paper cups. They were works of art. The chocolates may all have been rich brown on the exterior, but inside they hid varied surprises. Some were filled with peppermint, others with peanut butter or maple cream. Some had cherries nestled within, while others contained fluffy marshmallow or coconut. There were other kinds of candy too: striped ribbon candy, fudge, lollipops, licorice, rock candy, and jujubes.

Behind the scenes was fascinating to me. The large kitchen was always bustling. Greek words and accents were punctuated by clanging pots and dishes. The room in the very rear of the premises was the most secret and enticing. That barrel-filled room was where the candy was made. Pete was the head candy maker, and he took his work very seriously. He rarely smiled and never shared his candy-making recipes.

Although Pete appeared a little unfriendly, he was kind to me. I think that was because he could tell that I was enchanted by what he did.

"What is in these barrels and casks, Pete?" I ventured one day.

"Ahhh, in those barrels are the keys to our wonderful candy," he said with pride and a heavy accent.

Pete proceeded to lift the lids and show me the treasures hidden inside. There were casks of sugar, cocoa, and salt. Peanut butter, raspberry creme, lemon creme, and marshmallow were among the contents of some of the barrels. It was heavenly back in that room.

"And," he winked, "there are even more barrels stored downstairs."

Down a narrow staircase lay the cool recess of a basement. It was dim down there with just a single bare light bulb illuminating the area. But I could see that the cellar was packed with supplies: milk, meats, butter, and plenty more barrels.

A door from the candy kitchen led to a back alley. There Pete and some of the other cooks fed the alley cats our leftovers.

"It is good to have the cats around," explained Pete. "They keep the mice and rats away."

Several cats regularly stopped by for feedings. But there were some favorites who were even given names. There was a large orange cat who was called Flash because his bright fur was a flash of sunshine, and he was very fast. Flash seemed to be an astute cat who did not miss much action.

There was a beautiful white cat named Angel that Mr. Lindrokis himself was very attached to. During his evening break, Mr. Lindrokis would sit on a bench in the alley and gently stroke Angel. He would whisper softly to her. He loved that cat. Angel was a constant fixture at the back door. I think Angel became emboldened because she used to sneak inside. I always knew when Angel slinked in because loud exclamations in Greek would come out of the candy kitchen.

"Angel, you snoop around too much!" Pete would yell at her. "Don't you ever hear, 'Curiosity killed the cat'."

One day I arrived at work to find Mr. Lindrokis extremely distraught.

"What is the matter with our boss?" I asked Katherine.

"Oh," she said, "he can't find that white cat. Apparently the cat's gone missing for three days now."

Three days turned into four...then five...then a week...then a month. With the bustle of the job, I actually quite forgot about the beautiful feline.

One evening a month or so later, I was alerted to a major commotion emanating from the candy kitchen. Pete was screaming and crying, mostly in Greek. When I reached the doorway to this back room, Pete had his hands on the sides of his head and an incredulous look on his face.

"I don't believe it!" he cried, pointing to a large barrel.

Pete had been making marshmallow-filled chocolates that day and had reached the bottom of the barrel of marshmallow...only to find fluffy white fur.

Main Street East from Franklin Street

Chapter Nine
1922

"Rette deine seele...Rette deine seele," Papa sang.

"Papa, isn't that what Mrs. Barend always yells at Hans?" I asked.

"Yes, my Doll, it is. Rette deine seele means *save your soul*. And that's what I am doing now," he chuckled, "saving your soles."

Papa, who could do everything well except play the organ, was repairing our shoes. He sat at the table in the basement kitchen surrounded by leather, string, and various small metal tools. Papa truly seemed happiest when he was busy making or fixing something. And our shoes frequently needed fixing. The long walk into downtown reeked havoc on our soles and heels.

Downtown sat in a valley, and we had to climb the high Prospect Hill. Once near the top, we turned from the main road to reach our house. Our house was located near the bottom on the other side of the hill. So the walk into town really was uphill both ways.

Hans, who was now eleven years of age, slunk in the basement door. He looked surprised to see Papa and me there. I noticed that Hans often used the basement door when he wanted to avoid detection.

Hans wore a beige cap, and he had that cap pulled way down over his forehead. He was quickly making his way toward the stairs when I said, "Hey, not so fast. Men should not wear hats inside. It is not good manners." I grabbed his cap and snatched it off his head.

"Hans, what happened?" I cried. His forehead was brushburned.

"Nothing!" Hans insisted as he ran from the room.

"Come back! I can clean the wound for you!" I called to empty space.

The one good thing about Hans, I guess, is that he always got caught in whatever "errors in judgment" he made. To my knowledge, he never got away with anything. Rudi was able to pry out the truth. Hans had crashed a bicycle into a brick wall.

"Where did you get a bicycle?" Ted asked.

"I borrowed the bicycle," was Hans's reply.

Everybody else called it stealing a bicycle.

"Where did you take the bicycle from?" Papa inquired.

"Just down the hill a ways." Hans continued to be vague.

"Exactly where?" was the next question.

Extricating this piece of information required further probing...and threats of meal withholding from Lottie.

We came to learn that Hans "borrowed" the bicycle that was parked along the side of Our Lady of Mercy Church. We came to find out that the bicycle belonged to Father Mullane himself, and Hans had crashed into Father Mullane's church.

Our Lady of Mercy Church was an imposing Catholic church constructed of dark brick that sat about half way down the hill leading to the city. We attended Zion Lutheran Church, and Our Lady of Mercy was like foreign territory for me.

It was Rudi who marched Hans and the slightly bruised bicycle down to Father Mullane. Hans returned home with a long-term, non-paying maintenance position at Our Lady of Mercy Church.

"Oh, well," Papa tried to reason, "it will be good experience for you...And you'll be in good hands."

My job at Elites was going quite well. I was still waitressing the lower, center tables; but I worked hard and got better.

One day Mr. Lindrokis called me into his little office. He sat behind the roll-top desk looking rather forlorn. I think he was still grieving the loss of Angel.

"Crystal," he said. "You a hard-working girl. You do good job.

The customers, they like you. You now work the upper tables."

With that speech, I was elevated to the tables on the mezzanine. I was quite thrilled. And I was shocked when a short time later I was moved to the candy counter. That was a big promotion. Plus, the candy was my favorite part of the job anyway.

The candy counter consisted of a great length of dark wood along the top with sloping glass panels in the front. Pieces of wood that slid open and closed fit into the back side. Inside the candy counter were three tiers of shelves. Each shelf held trays of various candies. A large silvery scale was positioned on top of the counter.

Behind the candy counter were shelves reaching up to the ceiling. These shelves contained boxes and baskets. Mr. Lindrokis had been right. It was a good thing I was tall. I could reach the top shelves with ease.

My responsibilities were many. Of course I had to wait on the customers, packing up their boxes of freshly-made candy as they wished. The boxes were embossed with *Lindrokis's Elites* in blue ink. Each completed box was tied up with string. Customers could select any type of candy they wanted, except for chocolates filled with marshmallow which had been discontinued for awhile.

After the store closed, I had to remove all the trays of chocolates and store them in the cool basement. Then I had to clean and polish the candy counter, inside and out. I kept the counter spotless.

The best time of the year at Elites was Easter. Pete started getting chipper at the beginning of Lent, and his contagious excitement built as Easter neared. Amazing chocolates emerged from the candy kitchen. There were bunnies done in dark, milk, white, and even pink chocolate. There were eggs of all sizes filled differently. Some eggs were solid chocolate. Others were filled with coconut, peanut butter, nuts, and various creams. There were chocolate chicks and jelly beans. Chocolate crosses were framed in filigree designs. Each piece was like a little sculpture. I don't know how Pete did it.

Customers started placing their orders for Easter baskets and boxes in the weeks prior to the holiday. It became my job to keep track of the orders.

My favorite part of the Easter preparations was packaging the baskets. Paper grass was laid at the bottom, and the containers were then just loaded with goodies. After each basket was filled, I cut a giant piece of cellophane. The basket was placed on the center of the shiny wrap. I then drew up the sides of the wrapping and tied it together with a big pastel bow.

By Easter, the candy counter looked amazing. The top of the counter, as well as the shelves behind the counter, were heaving with festive baskets in fresh, clear wrap. Ribbons of pink, lavender, butter yellow, baby blue, and mint green resembled a flower garden. We all felt proud of our work and of the store.

Our relationship with Max continued to grow. Lottie and I looked forward to his visits. His wife Frieda was pleasant, and we really loved Milo, the baby. I enjoyed hearing about Max's job. He was working construction and would tell us about the projects he was busy with.

"I'm so glad Max is not working in the mines," Frieda said. "Working above the ground is so much safer."

Mining disasters were nothing new around here, but Frieda was referring to the latest catastrophe. The headlines read that seventy-eight miners were dead and thirty-three were injured at a mining disaster in the nearby community of Spangler.

I, too, was glad that Papa and my brothers worked above ground.

Chapter
Ten
1923

When Max started working, he gave Lottie, Hans, and me gifts. His gifts were unlike Otto's presents from Korea. Otto gave us porcelain dolls and pearl rings, which we deeply appreciated. But Max's gifts were different. He gave us the best books, classic novels and fine books of poetry. He encouraged us to read and improve our minds.

Max also volunteered at the local school, assisting with athletic coaching. He was quite a hit with the students and teachers. Max was a confident speaker and had the kind of personality that made him popular. He was entertaining.

We would go see the construction projects Max worked on. He was on a team that built a pretty little church in Summerhill. Max was proud of that job.

That year I graduated from high school. I'll never forget the new outfit I was awarded in honor of my graduation. Papa told Lottie and me to shop at the Penn Traffic Company, the finest store in town. Lottie made most of my dresses, which were just as lovely as anything in a store. But it was a rare treat to go in a fancy store and buy a new dress. I wanted Lottie to go with me, of course. Lottie wanted to go to examine the latest styles. She could commit details to memory and sew dresses without patterns.

We searched and searched. Finally, we settled on a wispy summer dress in pale yellow. It featured a square neckline and short sleeves. A belt of the same sheer fabric cinched my waist. The delicate material cascaded below my knees. Lottie, who inherited good taste from our mother, insisted on a white cloche hat with a tiny bow on the side and a brim that covered my forehead. My clunky feet, which I always felt were far too large, looked a bit daintier in white, strappy sandals. A pearl necklace of Mama's was the finishing touch.

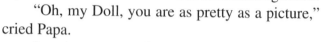

"Oh, my Doll, you are as pretty as a picture," cried Papa.

Imagine my surprise when a newspaper photographer actually snapped my picture wearing this ensemble. My photo was in *The Johnstown Tribune*!

Graduating from school meant I could now work full-time at Elites.

Mr. Lindrokis called me aside and said, "I now give you promotion. You now be our bookkeeper. I give you raise too!"

Fifteen dollars a week! That was big, big money back in those days!

I rushed home and burst in the door. "You'll never believe what happened!" I gushed. "I got a promotion and a raise!"

Lottie gave me a big hug while the others expressed their congratulations.

Hans, who may have been feeling left out, said, "I got a promotion at the church too. Father Mullane is teaching me how to clean the altar and sacristy."

"Yea," added Rudi, "and I hear he's is going to give you a raise too."

"Really?" asked Hans. He was clearly excited.

"That's right," Rudi continued. "Father is going to double your current salary."

Everybody burst out laughing, except Hans. He wore a confused expression, apparently trying to figure out what he missed.

I started my new responsibilities at Elites. I still waitressed and worked the candy counter because the bookkeeping didn't take all day. I was glad because I really enjoyed working the candy counter. When I had to work on the accounting, I went into the little back office. The roll-top desk held a typewriter and a pen with an ink well. Slender slots lined the back of the desk and held envelopes, stamps, and rubber bands.

I worked hard all that summer. The Greek men who worked at Elites were all kind, but they were slightly flirtatious.

"Oh, it's just their nature. It's in their blood," my friend and co-worker Katherine advised.

So none of us girls took the looks and remarks of the Greek men seriously. We just brushed off their compliments good-naturedly. And, if I was truthful, I would have to admit some of their attention was flattering...although I would never admit it.

Nick, Mr. Lindrokis's brother, especially used to smile at me. I paid little attention. He was in his thirties, and I was eighteen. Nick was an old man.

Mother nature hit us with a stretch of terribly hot weather that summer. The humidity was so bad we could hardly breathe. We just felt sticky and irritable. I remember it was one of those days when nothing was going right. The waitresses dropped dishes while the customers complained that the ice cream was melting too fast. The large ceiling fans stirred the air like hot soup but did little to provide us with relief.

I was mopping my brow with a handkerchief when Mr. Wilson, a regular customer, barged in and hurried to me.

I was surprised when Mr. Wilson grabbed my hand and pulled me aside. He said, "Crystal, I'm so sorry...so terribly sorry...There's been an accident."

I could only stare at him.

He licked his parched lips and swallowed. Still holding my hand, Mr. Wilson continued, "I've just come from Saint Michael."

Max and Frieda lived near the small community of Saint Michael, and Max was working on a construction project there.

"There has been an accident," Mr. Wilson repeated. "A terrible accident."

I stared at Mr. Wilson.

"Max was working high above ground. There was some problem with the wiring. He was electrocuted and fell to the ground." Mr. Wilson paused for a long time. "Crystal, Max is dead."

We were all in a state of shock. Max, tall and handsome...Max, honest and open...Max, the life of any party...Max, funny but also deep...Max, devoted husband and father...Max, dead at the age of twenty-eight.

It was a bright, sunny day when we traveled to Grandview Cemetery, this time by automobile.

"He's with Mama now," Hans said, for once making a contribution that was sensitive and appropriate.

I went about my duties feeling numb for quite awhile. Steamy summer rolled into crisp autumn, and the holiday season drew near. Late one gray afternoon, Nick pulled me away from the candy counter where I was boxing peppermint drops and candy canes.

"Crystal," he said with a smile, "please...come. I have a gentleman I want you to meet."

Nick escorted me back to the little office where I was introduced to Mr. Roland, owner of Roland's Jewelry. Roland's Jewelry Store was located across the street.

"Please, Crystal," Nick said, "make a selection...as a Christmas present."

With those words, Nick left Mr. Roland and me together.

"Please sit down," said Mr. Roland.

A black leather case sat in front of Mr. Roland. He unsnapped the top and slowly drew out a tray. I was wide-eyed. Nestled in furrows of black velvet were rows and rows of rings. I couldn't think.

"Take your time, Miss, and look. We have the finest selection of rings in town," boasted Mr. Roland.

My eyes traveled to the two rows closest to me. Diamonds! All diamonds. Blindingly bright diamond rings. My head was swimming. What could this mean?

Quickly I shifted my gaze to the other rows. The rows farther back contained colored gemstones.

"Thank you, Mr. Roland," I managed, "but I really am not in need of a ring at this time."

"Oh, but Mr. Lindrokis insists," stated Mr. Roland. "Come, take a look at this beauty." He gently removed a marquise-cut diamond.

"Ahhh...thank you...but I'd rather not," I stammered.

"Oh, but you must, my dear. Mr. Lindrokis insists, and he would be very disappointed if you did not select a ring." This guy was good. Mr. Roland was a professional salesperson who was not going to take no for an answer.

"But I can't...it's...it's too extravagant," I reasoned.

"How about this one?" Mr. Roland suggested, this time holding up a sparkling emerald-cut diamond. "Would you like to examine it through my magnifying glass?"

"Oh, I know your stones are of the highest grade," I managed. "It's just that I wouldn't feel comfortable accepting so generous a gift."

"Mr. Lindrokis would not have arranged for me to come here if he did not want you to select a special gift," Mr. Roland insisted.

He was smooth, and he was not about to leave without making a sale. Mr. Roland glanced at his pocket-watch, which was of fine quality. I could tell he was growing impatient and wanted to return to his store. After all, it was the Christmas season, his busiest time of the year. I, too, was anxious to return to the candy counter. I still had three trays of candy canes to box.

I looked at the velvet tray, choosing to skip the two rows of diamond rings. I focused on the colored gemstones. There were emeralds, rubies, sapphires, and opals. There were round cuts, square cuts, and marquise cuts. There were thick, smooth bands and bands with delicate filigree. I studied and studied. Mr. Roland cleared his throat and pulled out his watch a few more times. Finally I pointed to a ring in the back row. A round ruby sat in the center of a gold band. The ruby was surrounded by two small diamonds.

"Since I must choose something," I said, "I'll have that one."

"A lovely choice," said Mr. Roland, "although I think Mr. Lindrokis would have preferred a choice from the front rows."

Mr. Roland slid his velvet tray into his black leather case and went away. I politely thanked Nick for the Christmas gift, although I could not look at him in the eye. In fact, I avoided eye contact with Nick for most of the next year.

I couldn't wear a ring like that to work. It was impractical. My hands were always in something sticky.

When I got home, I told Lottie, but no one else, about the ring. I couldn't imagine telling my father about my gift. I didn't even want to keep the ring in my bedroom. Instead I dropped it in a rose-covered tea cup and placed the cup on the highest shelf of the cupboard. I never wore the ring.

Chapter
Eleven
1924

Nineteen twenty-four started out with a blast...in more ways than one. We experienced a blast of freezing, arctic air. The newspaper reported that in New York, a car was struck by a train at a railway crossing. Apparently, the railroad crossing gates had frozen and could not perform their safety function. *The Johnstown Tribune* also reported that a seventy-mile gale overturned another car. Inches of snow blanketed our area, which would cause problems later.

Sadly, in late January, another mine disaster was reported. This time, thirty-six miners in a neighboring community lost their lives. The details were heart-wrenching. *All of the victims were frightfully mangled by the force of the letgo...It is believed that one of (the miners) struck a sulphur streak and the sparks ignited a pocket of gas...When the body of John Hudak was found, his miner's lamp was burning and he still clasped his pick in his hand...Not far off were the bodies of John and Charles Crandell, father and son. They were lying side by side, as they worked...One victim, Chester Williams, a motorman, was so badly mangled that his identity was fixed only by a ring on one of his fingers and by the fact that several years ago he had a toe amputated. His widow made the identification...To add to the horror of the catastrophe is the fact that practically all the victims are married men, some of them with several children. Work has been slack and the company has been giving the married men first chance at what jobs offered.*

We forged through that frigid winter, looking forward to the spring. Little did we know spring would bring new challenges. The significant snowfall piled on the hillsides surrounding Johnstown. It kept on snowing well into March. The one bright spot was the hope of Easter. Pete had started making chocolate bunnies, crosses, and eggs, which was a sign that spring had to come. But March weather can be unpredictable. In one week we received four inches of snow by Thursday. On Friday, the sun shone brightly; and the temperatures rose to well above freezing. Everyone was happy to see the sun. Unfortunately, the warm sunshine meant that the snow melted rapidly. I woke on Saturday to gray skies. It rained for ten hours on Saturday.

The result was a rapid rise in the Stonycreek and Little Conemaugh Rivers. Residents of Johnstown become nervous when the rivers start to rise. The Great Flood of 1889 had left a permanent scar on the psyche of the city.

I sloshed through the streets to work that day and watched the unrelenting rain through the front door window. Unlike the rain, business was light that day. It was good that we had few customers because soon we were all needed in the basement. Water had started to seep into the cellar. A few inches had collected by noon. We scrambled to lift boxes, sacks, and barrels to higher ground. We filled buckets and dumped the water in the back alley. This went on all day. Pete was especially upset.

"Ahhh, my beautiful candy! It must be saved!" he cried with his hands on his head.

I worried as I'm sure we all did. Would this flood be as bad as the Great Flood? How much damage and destruction would be caused this time? And...would there be any casualties? We kept our thoughts to ourselves as we worked throughout the day.

Joy swept through the restaurant when Nick checked outside that evening.

"Praise God!" he cried. "The rain has stopped!"

Katherine and I hugged each other in relief. There was still more mopping to be done; but Mr. Lindrokis said, "Crystal. Katherine. You girls go home now. You check on your families."

The walk through town was not easy. Mud and debris covered the downtown streets. Many people were out cleaning up their stores and buildings. The walk got easier when I reached Prospect Hill. I was so anxious to reach home. Fortunately, our home was on high enough ground that it received no damage at all.

The photographs featured on the front page of the newspaper the next morning were shocking. The rivers that flowed through downtown were filled to the brim with just a few inches to spare before spilling over.

"We were protected," Papa said. "God has been good to us."

YMCA, Johnstown, PA

Perhaps because of the long, harsh winter or perhaps because we felt so grateful to escape a ravaging flood, the Easter season was more special than ever. Walking to work each day, I marveled at how the earth could awaken and blossom again after the terrible winter. Hyacinths and lilacs perfumed the air. Baby leaves in the freshest shades of yellowish-green dotted the trees. It was wonderful to be alive.

Also making the season special was Hans's Confirmation. Hans was thirteen now, and Rudi had insisted that Hans regularly go to classes for Confirmation. As most young boys did in those days, Hans dressed in suits with shorts. Wearing a suit of long pants was a big step into manhood. Rudi bought Hans a new suit for his Confirmation...with long pants. Rudi became Hans's hero.

Hans looked quite handsome in his new suit. He answered all of his questions correctly and was confirmed. We were proud of him.

"Maybe working at the church is rubbing off on him," Papa mused. Maybe.

Rudi got Hans to join the YMCA, and Hans was even considering scouting which was starting to take off in the area. The YMCA offered plenty of activities for young men. The building on Market Street contained basketball courts and an indoor swimming pool. There were rooms for training with barbells and even a shooting gallery where archery skills could be honed. Hans liked this room best of all.

The Johnstown Tribune, *March 31, 1924*

Downtown Johnstown's Central Park was lovely. Paths gently meandered through the park. Benches were scattered here and there inviting weary pedestrians to rest. Lush trees added shade in the summer and a palette of colors in the fall. The park also supported a sizable population of pigeons.

The pigeons in Central Park had been a source of controversy for the past decade. The birds even became a political issue. At one point, city officials wanted to completely rid the park of them. But there was a vibrant outcry from citizens who enjoyed the birds.

Residents were divided on the issue. Some said the birds were a dirty nuisance. These people felt the birds aggressively begged for food and left their mess behind. Pigeon supporters claimed that the birds were beautiful and added to the charm of the park. Personally, I didn't mind the pigeons; however, my friend Katherine was deathly afraid of them. She would take side streets out of her way to avoid walking near Central Park.

It was about this time that Hans and his buddies from the YMCA decided they were ready to field test their archery skills. Hans, who was lovable but did not always exhibit the best judgment, suggested Central Park.

"There are way too many birds there already," he reasoned.

The boys had downed about a dozen birds before Mr. McClusky, who was now a police officer, brought Hans home.

"What is this boy's punishment this time?" asked Papa tiredly.

"Nothing," said the policeman. Mr. McClusky was a long-time friend of the family and possibly still felt bad about Otto's cauliflower ear.

"Nothing?" questioned Papa.

"Nothing. I can't stand those filthy birds. Just last week I had to scrub the statue of Joseph Johns where those feathered menaces left their mark!"

Central Park

Chapter
Twelve
1925

Father Mullane had taken Hans under his belt, somewhat, which was good because Rudi moved away that year.

"Heaven help us!" exclaimed Lottie, turning her eyes to the sky.

It was Rudi who insisted that Hans go to school...both regular school and Sunday school. It was Rudi who got the truth out of Hans. It was Rudi who commanded Hans to face the people he wronged.

But Hans actually seemed to enjoy his maintenance position at the church. And, he was learning valuable skills. Father Mullane always had a job for Hans to keep him busy and out of trouble...for the most part.

Elites was as busy as ever. Mr. Lindrokis was in the process of opening another restaurant. The new business was called Lindrokis's Park Grill, and it was located on Franklin Street right across from Central Park. The new restaurant did not sale candy, but it did offer a splendid view of the park and the pigeons. The Park Grill served full meals. A huge window was at the front of the store, and directly inside the window was a gigantic grill. Passers-by on the sidewalk could stop and watch sausages, chicken, or even sunny-side-up eggs being prepared.

Customers flocked to both of Mr. Lindrokis's locations. I worked from early in the morning until after dark. Mostly I worked at Elites;

however, sometimes I was sent to work at the Park Grill. But I didn't mind. I was glad to be working.

Oh, mistakes were made. We were so busy that errors were inevitable. Pitchers of milk got dropped. Trays of candy tipped, depositing precious chocolates on the floor. And pots of soup got burned. So did dish rags and towels. We were always rushing about in the kitchen and dropping off our rags and towels. A few times a putrid scent filtered through the air. On these occasions, Pete would storm out of the kitchen holding a charred rag. With his dark brows drawn tightly, he would hold up the rag and scold us, "This is no good! You must be more careful!"

Exhausted, I trekked home one evening to find Hans and his buddies socializing on our porch. We had a large, wrap-around porch with a swing suspended at the far end. I could hear the boys laughing and carrying on from the top of Prosser Street. I descended our street, anxious to get home and get some rest.

"Hello boys," I greeted as I climbed onto the porch.

"Ha...ha...ha...he...he...he...hello to you too...ha...ha...ha," they simpered from the swing.

I dragged into the kitchen and plopped into the rocking chair. As I eased off my shoes, I said, "Lottie, I'm much too tired to deal with fourteen-year-old boys this evening. They're so loud. What are they up too?"

"I don't know," replied Lottie, looking tired herself. "I've been in here finishing up the dishes from supper....But I have to admit, I worry about Hans. Now that Rudi's gone, I hope Hans won't do anything foolish."

A few more times that summer I was greeted in a raucous fashion by Hans and his friends. I had an uneasy feeling that something wasn't right. But the fact was that I was away from the house for long portions of time. I was not around to watch Hans constantly. I told myself that Papa, Ted, and Lottie would keep a close eye on my youngest brother. And Father Mullane would be watching and guiding him too. Then I would feel a little better...for a little while.

Late one evening, I was reading a *Bible* passage in the parlor before retiring for the night. *Bible* reading was a habit Papa had instilled in me. I sensed a presence enter the room, and I looked up. Hans, looking rather sheepish, stood before me.

"Doll," he said.

"Yes, Hans," I responded.

"Doll...well...I sorta have a confession to make," stammered Hans.

I set down the *Bible*; then on second thought I picked it up again for strength.

"Oh, do you now?" I asked.

"Yea," he said, roosting on the edge of the green velvet couch. "Well, you know how I help out Father Mullane at Our Lady of Mercy?"

"Yes," I said.

"Well, Father has me doing all sorts of things down there. I sweep the floors and polish the pews. I shovel the walkways in the winter and rake the leaves in the fall. I even clean the sacristy where all the sacred vessels and the robes...and the wine are kept."

"What happened, Hans? Did you break something?" I asked. "We break dishes all the time at Elites. We just tell Mr. Lindrokis, and it's okay. People have accidents. He understands."

"I didn't exactly break anything," Hans said.

"Did you have an accident?" I pressed.

"Well, I didn't exactly have an accident either," he added.

"Hans, what did you do?" I asked.

He hesitated, then said, "Well, all that sweeping and raking makes a guy thirsty."

"I'm sure it does. Does Father give you water to drink?" I asked.

"Yes," Hans said, lowering his head, "but sometimes I help myself to his other beverages."

"Hans, you mustn't," I chided. "You must tell Father Mullane that you have drunk his milk or coffee."

"But I haven't drunk his milk or coffee," whispered Hans.

"Then what have you drunk? Tea? Juice?" I was losing patience.

"No. I borrowed wine...from the sacristy," was his reply.

"...Well, if I were you, I'd pray to Our Lady for plenty of mercy."

It was Ted's turn to march Hans down to Our Lady of Mercy

Church. Father Mullane was able to extract a full confession from Hans...Father was good at that. Apparently Hans initially took small sips of wine which grew into large sips over time. Eventually he would pour wine into a jar which he hid in his coat pocket. He replaced the missing wine with water. Hans was "smart" enough to leave enough wine in the original flask so the mixture still looked somewhat authentic. Then Hans would generously share the wine with his drinking buddies.

"That explains it," mused Father Mullane. "I thought I was being supplied with inferior wine."

Hans's latest escapade was serious. Not only did he steal...from a church. Not only was he drinking wine at the age of fourteen. But the Prohibition was on. In 1925, it was illegal to imbibe alcohol outside of religious services. People went to jail for that. Fortunately for Hans, he was a minor...not a miner.

Father Mullane and Papa met with Hans and talked to him. Hans promised he would never take the wine again. As punishment, Father assigned more jobs to Hans...but none in the sacristy.

One evening at Elites is seared into my memory. It was an especially busy evening. There had been a big football match. Many players and fans crowded into Elites following the game for sandwiches and sundaes. We couldn't move fast enough. We bumped into each other in the kitchen and tried to keep track of our customers.

The last patrons lingered until about eleven o'clock. After the final guests left, Mr. Lindrokis locked the front door. I was clearing off tables when I smelled a distinct odor. At first, I didn't pay much attention. I just assumed the smell was from the football players. The odor intensified, and the air became hazy. Suddenly, there were shouts from the back.

What happened next was a blur. Flames flared from the kitchen. Pete, Nick, and Mr. Lindrokis were shouting in Greek and whipping towels at the flames. I froze, not knowing what to do.

"Get out!!! Get out!!!" Mr. Lindrokis screamed.

Katherine and I along with some other workers unlocked the front door and rushed onto Main Street.

"Help!!! Help!!!" we cried.

In no time at all, flames were licking out the front door.

Katherine and I hugged each other. "Should we go back inside?" I cried.

"We can't," responded Katherine. "It's too hot." Indeed, the air rushing out of the door felt like a blast furnace from the steel mill.

Firefighters soon arrived and unraveled their hoses. They bravely blasted water into the blaze.

Katherine and I looked around. "Did everybody get out?" she asked.

We counted. All the waitresses and soda jerks were there. We were so relieved to see Mr. Lindrokis, Pete, and Nick rush toward us. They had escaped out the back door.

We huddled together in amazement. The scene before us was spectacular. Yellowish-orange flames climbed into the black sky. The roar was like a waterfall. The courageous firemen ventured inside to continue their work. We waited and waited. Finally, the orange flames were replaced with dark smoke.

We waited and waited some more. The fire fighters emerged.

"Mr. Lindrokis," the chief said. "Please accept our condolences on the loss of your building. Fortunately, there were no casualties."

"Thank you so much for stopping the fire," wept Mr. Lindrokis.

"We did have an interesting experience inside your building," said the chief. "In all my years of fire fighting, I have never seen such a thing. Some of my men and I went down in the basement because the fire had spread down there. After we extinguished the flames, we found ourselves in pitch black. We could not find the stairs and could not see a way out. We could not even see our hands in front of our faces. Fire was still raging above; so we knew we were in a death trap. Suddenly, we saw two small flashes floating in the dark. We followed the flashes. The flashes led us to the steps. The flashes were the eyes of an orange cat that was sitting on the steps. Mr. Lindrokis, that cat led us to safety. That cat saved our lives!"

The next morning we awoke to see the picture of Flash, the orange alley cat, on the front page of *The Johnstown Tribune*. Flash was being hugged by Fire Chief McGinnis and was dubbed a hero.

Chapter
Thirteen
1926

Flash went to live with Captain McGinnis, and Elites was rebuilt. It took most of the year to refurbish the candy store; and during those months of remodeling, I worked at the Park Grill.

When Elites reopened, I thought it was even prettier than before. There were still many beveled mirrors, but now there were booths with red leather cushions along the walls. Tall pillars of dark wood separated the booths. Updated cafe tables completed the center. Crystal chandeliers reflected light. The new candy counter was the largest in town, even bigger than the candy counters at the Penn Traffic Company or Glosser Brothers Department Store.

Unfortunately, there was another mine disaster in the area. This time in nearby Clymer. This time forty-four lives were taken. Mixed in on the front page of *The Johnstown Tribune* with the gruesome details of the mangled bodies of the entombed miners was an article out of Philadelphia which provided some comic relief.

The much-discussed crime wave may be attributed to bad teeth in the opinion of Dr. Jacob G. Tilem, of the city, attending the International Dentists' Congress here this week. There is a great preponderance of dental irregularities among prisoners in penal institutions, according to statistics, Dr. Tilem said, and he believed this to be a logical deduction that defective teeth may be linked up with the criminality of these individuals. Men whose teeth give them a hideous appearance, commonly called "buck teeth," naturally develop a grudge against society, Dr. Tilem said, resulting in acts of violence and other instances of law breaking.

"Well, at least Hans has straight teeth," Lottie chuckled.

Motorcycles had been around Johnstown for a good decade or so. At first they resembled bicycles with a small motor attached. They changed as the years went by. Some even had sidecars. By 1926, motorcycles were serious pieces of machinery. The engines were much bigger, and the gas tanks were shaped like teardrops.

My brothers loved motorcycles, but Ted was the first to save enough money to buy one. That motorbike rode Ted to work and back. Ted was generous about giving rides on his motorcycle. Many times I perched sidesaddle on the back of his bike and held onto his waist as we flew down Prospect Hill to Elites.

Ted had sacrificed for a long time to buy that motorcycle. He quit going to picture shows and the race track. He wouldn't buy new shoes or take his meals outside the house. Ted was proud of that bike.

By 1926, the decade was in full swing. Jazz magically pulsated out of radios. It was now acceptable to wear dresses to just below the knee. The new styles were much more comfortable, especially for us working girls. We could move about with greater ease.

Hairstyles were changing too. I remember Mama always had her long, wavy hair coiled in a bun. Now, women were cutting their hair. It was a radical change.

One day Katherine visited Lottie and me.

"How hot it is!" exclaimed Lottie, pushing aside wisps of hair from her forehead.

"Girls," said Katherine. "Do you know what we should do?"

"What?" I asked.

"Cut our hair!" she said enthusiastically.

"No! We can't," I maintained.

"Why not?" continued Katherine. "I'm tired of my cootie garages."

Katherine's long brown hair was gathered by her ears, and 'cootie garages' was the nickname given to her earphone hairstyle of the time.

Katherine went on, "Our long hair is a nuisance with our jobs. We're always tying it up to keep it out of the way."

"Do you think Mr. Lindrokis will allow it?" I asked.

"Why not? I think he will like it. After all, the shorter styles will be more sanitary for working with food."

Lottie and I himmed and hawed. We weren't sure we were ready for such a bold move.

"Tell you what," Katherine suggested. "Let's just go into Rose's Beauty Parlor and talk with her."

So, we trepidly ventured into the beauty parlor. Rose showed us the latest short haircuts. The latest styles included the imposing Shingle and the wavy Poodle. The elaborate Bubble cut required use of the permanent wave machine.

Katherine was the first to take the plunge. She opted for the Eton crop. Rose snipped and snipped. The result was very flattering on Katherine's chestnut hair.

Lottie and I looked at each other. Lottie was the brave one who stepped up next.

"I'll take a Bob." Lottie sounded confident. Lottie, too, stepped down from Rose's chair looking very good, sophisticated even.

I stalled as long as I could and finally said, "I'll take the cut you gave Lottie."

I sat in the chair, and Rose blanketed me with a cape. She combed out my hair, and I couldn't watch. My eyes were closed during the entire haircut. I heard the clipping of the scissors and felt hairs fall on my substantial nose.

"Okay, Crystal," said Rose, "Open your eyes now, and see how you like it."

First I looked at Rose, who was smiling. A good sign. Then I looked in the mirror not recognizing the girl who stared back. Except for the big nose, the girl looked cute. I shook my head. The loose hair swung against my neck. I felt free.

Motorcycles also make people feel free. That's part of their appeal. Motorbikes invite people to ride them. They tempt. They tease. They entice. They lure. And Hans could not resist Ted's motorcycle.

It was a strange coincidence of fate that Hans crashed once again into Our Lady of Mercy Church. This crash was scary because parishioners were congregating for Mass at the time.

"You must like it here, Hans," said Father Mullane dryly.

During next Sunday's Mass, Father Mullane reverently announced the prayer intentions. He prayed for the sick and the dying. He prayed for the hungry and impoverished close at home and in far-off lands. He prayed for Mayor Shields and President Coolidge.

Finally, Father Mullane said, "And let's add a special prayer of thanksgiving that no one was injured when Hans Edelweiss crashed his brother's motorcycle into the church. Had the vehicle veered otherwise, numerous parishioners could have been injured, maimed, or killed. Amen."

Chapter
Fourteen
1927

In 1927, we were mesmerized by the daring flight of Charles Lindbergh all the way across the Atlantic Ocean to France. We studied maps and tried to picture his trip. It was amazing to consider. Lottie, Katherine, and I studied his handsome face in the newspapers. He was amazing to consider.

In 1927, a flight of a different sort also occurred.

"Hans! Hurry for breakfast!" Lottie called loudly up the steps.

I was setting the table while Lottie was making my favorite breakfast, Crepe Suzettes. She rolled out the dough so thin it was translucent. Then she coated the dough with butter and fried each circle of dough in a pan. Lottie flipped the thin dough with ease. I could never flip Crepe Suzettes without mutilating them. When each pastry was perfectly cooked, Lottie filled them with whatever fruit was available and rolled them into an egg roll shape. For the final step, she sprinkled the Crepe Suzettes with fine powdered sugar. They were scrumptious.

"Hans! You're going to be late again! Father Mullane will be angry!" Lottie cried. "What in tarnation is keeping that boy?" she muttered to me.

After Lottie sugared the final Crepe Suzette, she tried once more, "Hans!! Get down here...NOW!!!" She was really cross.

"I'll run up and get him," I offered.

I bounded up the steps and knocked on the boys' bedroom. Hans and Ted were the only occupants of the large room at the time. And Papa and Ted left for work at the crack of dawn.

The Johnstown Tribune, *May 23, 1927*

"Hans?" I said, rapping again. There was silence.

"Hans? Are you in there? Are you all right?" I thought maybe he was ill.

I gently pushed open the door to find...no one. Ted's bed was neatly made. And Hans's blankets were crumpled in a nest. I rushed over to Hans's bed and shook his blankets. He was not buried underneath. I stood with my hands on my hips, looking completely around the room.

"Hans Herman Edelweiss," I commanded, "if you are hiding, come out. Honestly, you're too old to be playing these kinds of games."

There was no response. I checked the closet. No Hans. I peered under the beds. No Hans. I investigated the other bedrooms. No Hans. I even went into the attic. Still no Hans.

I too was cross as I stormed down the stairs. "Lottie," I sighed, "I don't know where your little brother is."

"Do you think he may have already risen to get an early start at the church?" Lottie asked.

We looked at each other and burst into laughter. We searched everywhere: basement, parlor, dining room, yard, and barn...although we did eat Crepe Suzettes in between...but there was no sign of Hans.

I helped Lottie clear up; then I had to go to Elites. Hans was on my mind throughout the day...more or less. Where could that boy be?

I was greeted by the sound of Lottie's crying when I arrived home that evening. Lottie never cried. She was sitting in the rocking chair in the kitchen with a lace handkerchief held up to her face. When she looked up, her eyes were blotchy. She must have been crying for some time.

"Lottie, dear," I soothed, kneeling by her side. "What's wrong?"

"It's Hans," she sobbed.

"What has he done now?" I asked.

"He's...he's run away!" Lottie wailed.

"Oh, Lottie," I asked, "are you sure?"

"Yes, Mrs. Harper was here most of the day," she said. The Harpers were neighbors; in fact, they were some of our nicest neighbors. "Hans ran away with Hughie Harper," Lottie continued.

"Lottie, are you sure?" I pressed.

Lottie explained, "Yes, Hughie was at least considerate enough to leave his mother a note. Doll, they plan to go to California!"

I gazed out the window at the horizon. "They'll never make it," I assured her.

After breaking the latest news to Papa and Ted, Lottie and I felt we needed to inform Father Mullane. We walked to Our Lady of Mercy Church with our arms linked and our faces downcast.

"Hello Father," said Lottie.

"Why, hello girls! Come in, come in! Have a seat," invited Father Mullane. "Why do you look so sad?"

"It's Hans. He won't be available for work. He...he has run away," I explained.

"Then why do you look so sad?" he repeated. Then he quickly added, "I'm sorry girls. This isn't the time for humor."

Father Mullane paced a little then sat on the edge of his sofa. "Girls," he said, "I know you are worried about your brother. And quite possibly you may even miss him, but I want you to know that I have seen this before...plenty of times. Teenage boys reach a certain age, and they become restless. They hear stories of great adventure and fortune in far-away places. They sneak out of their windows in the middle of the night. They make their way to the train tracks and hop a train. Girls, they always come back."

"But Father," asked Lottie, "what should we do?"

"Just wait for him. Oh, you might want to say some prayers while you wait," Father Mullane said, patting Lottie's hand. "And enjoy the peace while he's gone." Father winked. He continued, "Some people have to learn the hard way. He'll be back. Don't worry."

But Lottie did worry. I did as well, but Lottie had become the mother figure in our house. She felt responsible for Hans. Day after day Lottie sat in that rocking chair by the kitchen window and stared out, waiting for Hans. She rocked so much that I thought she was going to rock ruts through the blue and white linoleum tiles. Day after day Lottie wore a pensive, serious look on her face. Her usual smile and warm humor had dissipated.

Father Mullane visited us every day. He saw how Hans's latest escapade was wearing down Lottie.

"Girls," Father Mullane said, "I know just what you need!"

"What is that, Father?" asked Lottie.

Father answered, "You need to go to a football game!" He smiled and clapped his hands.

"A football game?" I asked.

"Why yes, of course!" said Father. "What could be better than a seeing a football game for getting some fresh air and taking your mind off your worries for a bit?"

Who could argue? Father Mullane was one of the sponsors of a neighborhood football team. The team was called the Prospect Gridders; and it was comprised of tough, young men. I had never attended one of their games, but they had a reputation for winning. So far this year, the Prospect Gridders had won eight games and lost just one. Their only loss was to the team from Park Hill. That was a sore spot for the football fans in the neighborhood. Their final game for the season was the next day.

Lottie and I looked at each other. "Okay," Lottie said. "We'll go."

"Fantastic!" said the good father. "I promise you, you won't regret it. It will be a life-changing experience for you!"

Prospect A. C.

We bundled up the next afternoon and made our way to the Prospect Field. A substantial crowd had already gathered. Lottie and I squeezed onto the wooden bleachers. No admission fee was charged, but a hat was passed around for donations. The football players had to provide their own uniforms and equipment. The donations helped the players out.

Soon the Prospect Gridders ran onto the field. They were clad in brown pants and close-fitting knit shirts. Those who could afford helmets wore them. The players did not wear much in the way of padding and the shirts were tight, so we could not help but notice that the players were muscular...very muscular. Not that we were trying to notice. It was just that the fabric the shirts were constructed from really gripped their bodies.

...Anyway, the Prospect Gridders clobbered the team from Morrelville. The athletes ran up the field and down the field. They made amazing catches. They tackled and threw their opponents down like sacks of potatoes. At times I couldn't watch, but yet I did. It was brutal...yet exciting.

Afterwards, Father Mullane caught sight of Lottie and me. "I'm so glad you girls could make it," he smiled. "So...what did you think?"

"It was thrilling," said Lottie.

"Very action-packed," I added.

Some of the players were exiting the field and saying their good-byes to Father Mullane.

"Great game, boys! Great season!" praised Father as he patted the passing players on their broad shoulders. "Oh, Yock! I'd like you to meet these fine girls."

A tall, stocky youth smiled. He combed his fingers through his thick brown hair.

"Yock Reynolds," Father Mullane introduced, "I'd like to make you acquainted with Crystal Edelweiss." I nodded. "And her sister Charlotte."

Father continued, "Now, this strapping young man's real name is George. Some day he will have to tell you how he earned the nick-name 'Yock'."

Yock stared at Lottie, "Could I visit you sometime and tell you the story?"

Lottie blushed.

George...I mean Yock...started frequenting 413 Prosser Street with some regularity. Mostly he and Lottie sat in the parlor and talked. At first Yock intimidated me. He was so big and tough looking. And he often wore such a serious facial expression. My impression of him changed completely as I got to know him better.

I learned that this strong football-playing steel worker could play *Rhapsody in Blue* and other Gershwin tunes on the harmonica. He was also an impressive tapdancer. Despite his size, Yock was surprisingly light on his feet. He loved to deal black jack and play checkers. I never could beat him at checkers. And, he was an artist of sorts. A blackboard hung in our kitchen. I'd come home from Elites and always know if Yock had been there. He would leave pictures on the blackboard. They were caricatures really, of cows or ladies with big hats and handbags.

His works of art brought smiles to our faces. Which was what we needed, especially Lottie. It had been weeks, and still we had received no word of Hans.

Yock tried to brighten our days and distract us with jokes.

"Hey, Doll, do you know what that big, fat butcher down at Penn Traffic weighs?" Yock would ask.

"About 250 pounds?"

"No...pork!" And he would laugh and laugh.

Once Yock told me of a theft. Two friends of his boarded a train. A short while into the journey, one of the men discovered he had lost his pocket watch. The pocket watch was a very special family heirloom. The men searched everywhere. They looked under the seats and in the cushions. They checked the storage compartments. Other passengers, and even the conductor, joined in the search. Still the watch remained missing. At dinnertime, a steward wheeled a shiny cart of food down the aisle. The two men bought sandwiches. One of the men opened his sandwich.

"Doll, guess what he found inside?" asked Yock.

"The watch!" I enthused.

"No...ham!"

I fell for his jokes all the time. Yock loved food, and it showed in his humor.

"Lottie," I asked, "exactly how did Yock get that nickname?"

"He told me that when he was a kid, a wagon carrying cabbage often passed down his street. He and his friends would try to jump on the back of the cabbage wagon as it rolled by. Invariably his friends would fall off, but George always managed to hang on for a long ride. The kids started calling him Yock. 'Yock' means 'cabbage' in the old country."

I wasn't surprised to learn that even his nickname was food related. Yock loved good food. Lottie loved to prepare good food. They seemed to go together...like pork and sauerkraut.

Weeks transpired. Still there was no sign of Hans. Lottie continued to carve ruts in the linoleum with the rocking chair. One day

Lottie was looking out the window for Hans...and she saw him walking down the street!

She rushed out and met him. He was thinner. He was dirtier. He was possibly taller. He was missing a finger. Hopefully he was wiser. But he was Hans!

We were all happy to have him home. Papa welcomed him back like the Prodigal son. We didn't pry at first, wanting to let the boy settle in a little. But finally, we couldn't stand it anymore.

"Hans, where did you go?" asked Lottie.

While filling up on one of Lottie's savory meals, Hans told us that he and Hughie Harper hopped a freight train in Johnstown and headed West.

"Hans, what happened to your finger?" Lottie persisted.

"Well, Hughie and I had to change trains every once in awhile. We were out West a ways when we had to make a switch. It was dark. Hughie managed to jump on board with no problem. I followed him. As I stepped up on the ledge, I knew something was wrong. I reached up with my hands to grab hold of the door. Next thing I knew I was flat on my back. A man had shot me for trespassing...right in the finger."

"What happened then?" I asked.

"Well, when the guy saw how young we were, I guess he felt bad because he took me to a doctor."

"Son, you were lucky, my boy," Papa said. Then he added sadly, "I suppose this means I will never teach you how to play that beautiful instrument, the organ. My son, you were my last organ-playing hope. But I do hope you learned a thing or two from your experiences."

We all hoped Hans had learned much.

Chapter
Fifteen
1928

Hans had learned plenty. Over the years, he had learned to be daring. He had learned to be a good talker. And, he had learned to be charming.

Although Hans got into trouble a lot, everybody liked him. There was something about his personality that you could not resist liking. Nobody could stay angry at him for long. I really don't know how he did it.

Hans was growing up. He was now as tall as any of his older brothers. There were signs too that he was growing inwardly.

He had obtained his first, of many, paying jobs. It was at the city incinerary. That was where the rubbish of the city was burned. Personally, I couldn't imagine working in a place that scorching.

Mrs. Barend had her own opinion. "That is a good place for him. He'll have to get used to the heat for where he is headed," she prognosticated, nodding her head in confidence.

I was shocked when Hans handed me twenty dollars, his first pay.

"No, Hans. I can't possibly take your first pay," I choked.

"You must, Doll. You've given me so much," he said. "It's the least I can do."

I was touched.

I was less touched by the giggling girls who came into Elites. "Are you Hans's sister?" they chirped.

"Yes." I shouldn't have admitted it.

"Oh, he's sooo dreamy!"

"He's such a doll!"

"He's as cute as a button!"

"He has the most unusual eyes! They're speckled gray."

"No...they're more steel blue."

"I think you are both wrong. Hansy's eyes are more of a gray-green."

"He has bedroom eyes!!"

"And, he can dance the Charleston better than any fella in town."

"I think he's better at the Black Bottom."

"Well, I like to watch him dance the Shimmy!"

"And, he's so courageous!"

"He's such a dare devil!"

"Well, he's certainly the last part," I said under my breath. Escorting the young flappers to the door, I managed to say, "It was lovely to meet you girls. Do stop back again."

"Hansy??? Bedroom eyes???" Lottie reacted. "Heaven help us! And where did he learn all those dances?"

But Lottie had other things besides her little brother on her mind...like preparing for her wedding. Of course, she sewed her own wedding gown as well as my bridesmaid dress. Of course, the dresses were gorgeous. Lottie's gown was of ivory satin. Mine was of pale periwinkle blue with a dropped waist. Oh, she made her own wedding cake too.

Just prior to the wedding, Hans sought me out.

"Oh...umm...Doll," he said.

"Yes," I replied.

"Do you remember that twenty dollars I gave you?" he asked.

"Yes," I replied.

"Umm...well...I need to buy a wedding present for Lottie and Yock...and some other things..." he stammered. "Well...you don't suppose I could borrow it back?"

"Tell you what, Hans," I said. "You may have it back. Just make sure you get Lottie and Yock a memorable gift."

The wedding was full of warmth and love. Yock came from a large Irish, Catholic family. We were Lutheran, but my father accepted the arrangement. Attitudes were opening up in the 1920's. Plus my father really liked Yock and respected Father Mullane. But to be quite honest, after Otto married his cousin, just about any marriage between non-relatives would have been seen favorably in our family.

Hans almost didn't make it to the wedding. According to his side of the story, he was working hard at the incinerary. He became so hot that he needed a break. He needed fresh air. So he left work and borrowed a co-worker's convertible. He took it for a ride. The problem was that Hans had never driven an automobile before. He crashed into some bushes. Hans again was lucky. The car sustained minor scratches; however, Hans had to face the police. They called it stealing a car. Hans ended up paying a heavy fine. That was Hans's memorable wedding present to Lottie and Yock.

After the wedding, Lottie and Yock moved into a little house that had been built at the back of our property. We were all glad they remained close by.

The young newlyweds were just settling in when the neighborhood became abuzz with excitement. Another football season was about to begin. The Prospect Gridders had a great season the previous year, but the team had lost one game to Park Hill. They were determined to win against that team this year.

Prospect Field was packed for the match-up against Park Hill. Soon the action began. None of the Prospect players seemed to go by their baptismal names. Brute McKendree ran in for the first touchdown. The crowd exploded. Webb O'Donnell, who could catch anything, snagged a high pass from Bull McDonald to place the Gridders on the five yard line. It was Lefty Hands who sealed the victory with another touchdown. The final score was Prospect 14; Park Hill 0.

It was a very good year.

Johnstown Police Force, December 3, 1903

Epilogue

On a pleasant spring day in 1929, Lottie and I were strolling downtown. We were making our way to Glosser Brothers Department Store to buy pink and blue yarn. Lottie and Yock were expecting a baby. Of course, Lottie was making all the baby's blankets and clothes.

"Look at that new business," I pointed out. The door was open on the warm afternoon, and the sound of tapping greeted our ears. A sign out in front of the building read *The Gene Kelly Studio of the Dance*. Gene Kelly was a young local dancer who was just starting out.

"Oh," Lottie said, "Mrs. Barend predicts nothing will come of him."

We continued on. The trees in Central Park were blossoming in vibrant shades of pink and white. Tulips lined the walkways. The pigeon population seemed scaled back. Church bells sang through the air. Joseph Johns's head glistened brightly in the sunshine.

Central Park

A young couple approached us. The boy looked familiar.

"Lottie," I whispered, pulling her closer. "Look ahead."

"Why...it's Hans," she replied. "Who's he with?"

"I don't know," I confessed.

"Let's find out!" Lottie was determined.

I could have sworn that Hans saw us and quickly averted his gaze. He took a pretty girl by the arm and started her on a path away from Lottie and me.

Lottie called out, "Hans! Oh Hans!!"

Lottie's voice could carry when she wanted it to.

The pretty girl turned and whispered to Hans. He was caught. He would have to face us. Soon Lottie and I met up with the young pair.

"Oh, hello Hans!" called Lottie.

"Um...hi." Hans was demure.

I got a good look at the girl. She was very pretty with blond hair, blue eyes, and dimples. She was so young. She couldn't have been more than sixteen. But she seemed to be very happy, glowing even.

"Lottie...Doll, I'd like you to know Louise," introduced our brother. "Lousie, please meet my sisters, Lottie and Doll."

"So nice to meet you," said Lottie, extending her hand. I could tell Lottie was inspecting the girl as much as I was.

Suddenly Louise gushed, "Oh, look at the beautiful ring Hans just gave me!"

Louise proudly thrust out her hand. She was beaming. On her dainty finger rested a lovely ring. The gold band held a red ruby with two small diamonds on either side.

References for *Prospect Hill*

Richard Burkert. *Pictures From Our Past: A Visual History of Johnstown.* The Johnstown Area Heritage Association, 2000. (Place of Publication Unknown).

Lyndee Jobe Henderson and R. Dean Jobe. *Images of America: Johnstown.* Arcadia Publishing: Charleston SC, 2004.

Ed Kane with Elizabeth Rosian. "Central Park" in *Johnstown magazine*, Volume 1, Issue 3, pages 44-52, June 2005.

Judith Kinter. *King of Magic, Man of Glass: A German Folk Tale.* Clarion Books: New York, 1998.

Richard H. Mayer. *Historic Pages from Johnstown Newspapers.* Johnstown Flood Museum Association, Johnstown PA, (Date unknown).

Greg Nickles. *We Came to North America: the Germans.* Crabtree Publishing Company: New York, 2001.

Acknowledgments

The author is extremely grateful to Cover Studio for the use of the photographs from Johnstown's past and to *The Tribune-Democrat* for the use of the historic newspaper excerpts.

Cover background photo by Sergey Galushko, Ukraine
Chapter Head Photo by Alistair Scott, Switzerland

About the Author

Kimberly Seigh has worked as a social worker, primarily with the developmentally disabled. Serving as a Peace Corps volunteer, she worked in Uganda on an orphans' project. Most recently, she has been employed as a teacher of a variety of grades and subjects, with language arts being her favorite.

Kimberly lives with her husband and three cats in Pennsylvania where she enjoys hiking in the woods. She greatly enjoyed researching and writing *Prospect Hill* and is currently working on her next novel. She is a popular new addition to the Headline Books School Show Program and will be visiting school students bringing living history in the classroom.